The Labors of Herkimer
A Myth for Our Time

By

C. N. Blakemore

ISBN: 0-7596-6496-X

Library of Congress Control Number: 2002102126

This book is printed on acid free paper.

Printed in the United States of America
Bloomington, IN

1stBooks - rev. 1/14/02

I

Herkimer Hartland Hampton, commonly known as Banty, boarded the morning plane in Des Moines and headed East. This was to be a new and foreign experience to him. He had visited no states outside his native Iowa other than Missouri, Nebraska and Minnesota. He had never crossed, nor even seen, the Father Of Waters which graced the Eastern boundary of the Hawkeye State.

Herkimer was a true son of the soil. The town of his origin, Clayton, housed hardly two thousand humans, though vastly more animals of lower breeding; cows, pigs, chickens and sheep inhabited the farms in the undulant, verdant fields which surround Clayton and the other towns of southern Iowa. Indeed the name he answered to, Banty, was the farmers' debasement of Bantam rooster, a creature of minimal stature which would strut and crow in the henyard, daring other, larger fowl to challenge his right to first choice, perhaps the earliest evidence of machismo in The New World.

Herk's small stature had given rise to the name. As he boarded the plane he had achieved the age of sixteen and the height of five feet six inches and showed no promise of further growth. As antidote to this deficiency in his persona he had developed a powerful, albeit slight, frame. By the age of twelve when it became apparent that he would not match his associates in height he began to lift barbells, to ride his bicycle prodigiously and develop skills at football and baseball, as well as on the wrestling mat, which prevented any of his school mates from making direct challenge to him. He could throw a bale of hay higher than any of his fellow laborers in the blue-grass fields and was in demand at the seed company each August from age thirteen onward.

Now he was embarked on an enterprise completely alien to his previous existence. He had never been in a large airplane, only his uncle's small, four passenger model. In that he had felt free, exhilarated: he had a limitless purview of earth and firmament. In this monster he was enclosed, trapped. No view save the aisle described by the long rows of chairs on either side, the heads of other mortals, the stewardess—who, of all, was pleasing to contemplate—and the midget portholes. For he was placed at precisely the center of the ship, adjacent to the aisle.

He had experienced some embarrassment in boarding. He had insisted on carrying, clutched to his breast, his great grandfather's Civil War cavalry saber, a treasure of history entrusted to him by his grandfather as guardian of this family heirloom. There had been some question as to the propriety of, and the need to maintain, his personal guardianship of this quaint instrument on the plane. His pertinacity had prevailed and he was permitted, with the ascent of the kindly black man who sat next to the window of the row in which Herk settled, to store the yard long blade of steel in the space beneath the seats directly before them. This was just at the beginning of the tight security era and Herkimer's innocent attitude convinced the airline authorities that it would be a harmless act to relax their restriction and allow him passage with his sword.

Herkimer was, indeed, embarked on a new road in his life. One month shy of his fifteenth birthday his loving mother had died of vile cancer and something more than a year later his father had found it too exhausting a task, when measured with his position as Chief Justice of the Supreme Court of Iowa, to attempt, also, to provide guidance to a teenage son. Herkimer, being the sole heir to the Judge, needed, especially in his adolescence, closer supervision than the Judge could provide, so the elder Mr. Hampton had presumed upon his cousin, Mr. Joseph Wilson, a successful Wall Street investment banker and autocrat of a two member family, to oversee the further development of his younger son, Herkimer.

As Herk was born aloft and conveyed toward the rising sun he suffered conflicting sentiments: anticipation at the prospect of experiencing that part of society he had previously met only in books and on television; melancholy from the realization that he was severing direct connection with that life to which he had successfully adapted. His mother's death had left him, for months, with a strong malaise, but after a year the sorrow had miraculously lifted. His father, who had never been diligent in attention to his only child did not alter his habits; he traveled regularly to court sessions in the state capital, leaving Herk under the nominal supervision of a country lass scarcely seven years his senior and who expanded his education into the realm of sex. "Oh, Banty," she would cry as they disrobed before retiring, "you're so bee-ute-eeful," and this would be followed by an hour or more of athletic copulation in his mother's expansive four-poster. They were fortunate to cohabit during the seventh decade of the Twentieth Century when the Puritan morals prescribing abstinence—had they ever been so strictly observed as attested—were considerably relaxed. She spirited him, monthly, in her Jeep, across the border into Missouri, where he was unrecognized by the merchants, so that they might replenish, in the local pharmacy, his supply of condoms. Yes, young Herkimer, was loathe to leave his private paradise though he knew his relation with the young chaperone was a major topic of gossip, the primary mode of communication in a town such as Clayton where it was generally conceded that his suspected conduct with her was the cause of his banishment to the barren realm of Empire City.

This conjecture was true, for when the gossip eventually reached the Judge it was the final determinant in his decision to find firmer supervision for his offspring.

Before Herk left Des Moines the Judge had taken him aside in the Red Carpet Room at the airport for a short session of counsel. Judge Hampton had been of middle age when Herkimer came squalling into the world and was considerably older than most men who are parent to those in their teens. His hair was gray at the temple, receding from his forehead. The creases which descended from the corners of his eyes gave a serious aspect to his gaze though he was a man of high good humor who loved a fine yarn. He smacked his lips once as he was about to begin which gave warning that what followed was to be seriously considered

"Now, Son," the elder Hampton began, "you are leaving the relative peace and innocence of a pastoral community which is all you have ever known. You are going to the raucous and often bellicose life of the largest of our cities. You will, perhaps, be tempted on all sides by lust and greed. While you may have had a minor lapse in chastity I blame that on your youth and my own laxity. I have faith that you will maintain the moral values instilled in you by a sainted mother and have the utmost confidence that my cousin, Joe Wilson, and his fine wife will guide you as well as anyone I know.

"And always remember this, my son, which has been a code of ethics for all Hamptons—*your word is your bond.* Live by that and you will do no wrong whether you make mistakes or not. An honest mistake cannot hurt you; a deliberate lie can and ultimately will."

With that the father and son had embraced and the youth had departed for the gate fairly brandishing his warrior heirloom.

The initial minutes of Herk's journey on the mechanical bird were awkward; the other passengers studied him with curiosity as he placed his sword beneath the seats. It was not until the plane was in the sky that he was encouraged to relax by the energetic smile of the African American, a man in his late middle years who sat by the window, an empty chair between them.

"That's some weapon," the man said, his alabaster dentures gleaming.

"My Great Grandfather's Civil War cavalry saber," Herk answered.

"Civil Wa-ahr?" The man dragged the phrase into a question. "Which side?"

"The North," Herk hastened to answer. "The First Ohio Cavalry."

"The right side," said the man looking across at Herkimer from beneath eyebrows silver against the dark background of skin. "My kin fought, too. Same side."

Herk was surprised, puzzled. "I didn't know that any Negroes fought in the war."

"Most people don't. My kin fought out on the border country—in Kansas."

Herkimer said nothing more. He was, as yet, shy of strangers. After several minutes of silence his seat companion once again raised his head.

"My name is Ed Williams," he said.

"Pleased to meet you," said Herk. "My name is Herkimer Hampton."

"You're from the country, I can tell," Williams said in a friendly tone. "Have you ever been to the city?"

Herk was confused. Hadn't he just boarded this plane in the city. "Des Moines?" he questioned.

Williams' ivory grin stretched the muscles at his jaws. "Des Moines is a burg. I mean Chicago, Detroit, New York."

"I'm going to live in New York," Herk answered with assurance.

"Good." Williams seemed genuinely pleased, but his expression immediately turned severe. "You better watch where you carry that weapon of yours." He pointed to the floor. "Some places in the city they'll take it from you. Might even use it on you."

Herkimer was to recall these words as he paraded through the O'Hare Terminal from his carrier of arrival to his carrier of departure, his sword extended from his hand. He felt as though each individual he met or passed had eyes on the heirloom. As he sat at the gate waiting to board the flight to New York one burly fellow in particular kept casting glances at it and Herk was certain it was with covetous, rather than curious, intent.

He once again encountered reluctance on the part of the crew to allow him passage with sword in hand but he was surprised, at the moment he felt he was about to be denied his request to carry it with him, by the intrusion into the discussion of the same Mr. Williams who had been his seat mate on the previous flight.

"He doesn't pose any threat, folks," said the kindly gentleman. "He rode with me from Des Moines and we kept the sword on the floor under the seats in front of us. Just look at this young man. You can tell he's honorable. You let him sit in the seat beside me and we'll watch it together. That's a genuine heirloom and I understand why he's nervous about letting it out of his sight."

What Herk had not known was that Williams was an employee of the airline and so, after a considerable amount of discussion between the gate keepers and Williams, Herk was permitted to carry the saber aboard once again.

As they settled into their seats, sword stowed beneath their feet, Herkimer offered the man sincere thanks for his assistance. Before the flight was completed the crew would acknowledge a debt of gratitude even more genuine to Herk and Williams.

When the craft had ascended from Earth and attained cruising altitude Mr. Williams had, once again, opened a dialogue, this on the attractions and dangers of the City of New York. Midway through a sentence he paused in his discourse.

"Listen!" he said. "Did you hear some disturbance in the First Class section?"

As Herk and his fellow traveler looked to the curtain between sections they heard, definitely, some sounds of alarm. Though the **Fasten Seat Belts** signal was still aglow Herkimer flipped off his binding, arose and approached the divider between the two cabin areas. He carefully pushed aside, ever so slightly, the curtain and peeked through into the upper class area. An outrageous scene was revealed. There at the head of the aisle stood an angular, muscular, dark-haired woman, her blouse thrown open to reveal a torso garbed in a leather vest. Around her mid-section, on top of the vest, was wound a large, long serpent, evil tongue flicking as it hissed, held behind its large, flat head in the woman's hand, gloved in leather which extended to the elbow. She was pointing the beast directly at the two flight attendants who, Herk perceived, were backing toward the curtain behind which he stood.

"Vee are goink to Cooba!" screeched the woman, and, beckoning the attendants with her free hand, added, "Tell zee pilot!"

Herk's reaction was visceral and without thought. He stepped back, leaned down and retrieved his beloved sword, drew it from the scabbard and flung himself through the curtain into the first class section.

He stopped, sword raised. The attendants, already frightened and seeing the weapon, both emitted muffled screams and fell back into the passenger seats leaving the aisle free for Herk's passage.

The other passengers, terrified at the sight of the evil-looking snake, had drawn back toward the fuselage on either side. The threatening woman's face flamed with anger and she stepped forward shouting, "Damn you!"

That was to prove an error on her part for she placed herself in sufficient proximity that, with one sweep of the sword, Herkimer rendered her live weapon headless and impotent.

"Curse you!" she shouted as two men, one from either side of the aisle, seized her and forced her, face down, onto the aisle floor.

Herk stood looking down on the thwarted hijacker as she struggled for only a moment and then submitted to the two men who held her. He was seized with a powerful tremor but this was promptly relieved by the firm grip of a hand on his shoulder.

"Good work, my boy!" It was an accolade and Herk turned his head into the smiling face of Ed Williams. "I believe you have saved us all a bit of a detour."

The remainder of the flight was uneventful though a feeling of tension continued to pervade the ambiance. The wild woman was strapped to a seat in the forward section and, after she had shouted several epithets at the situation in general, her mouth was gagged with one of the flight attendant's scarves. Her grunts and groans continued as reminders of the dangerous incident until the wheels touched down, the airplane had taxied to the arrival gate and she was led from the cabin by the waiting policemen.

Waiting also, of course, were numerous purveyors of the news, some brandishing photographic equipment. In an effort to avoid these scavengers

Herkimer requested late exit from the craft. He was supported in this by his new friend, Ed Williams, who stayed behind with him until all other passengers had disembarked. Williams, sensing Herk's innocent reticence to celebrity entreated the flight attendants to allow them a few extra minutes in the safety of the cabin in hopes that the gossip sharks would feel they had enough of the details and depart, each in hopes of becoming the earliest to report on the high drama of the skies.

The plan nearly succeeded, but when Herk and Williams emerged from the gate followed by the last of the attendants one laggard camera person spotted the young man with the sword and caused a commotion, shouting and flashing his bulbs, so that the whole contingent quickly returned, and had Herk not been protected by the stalwart Mr. Williams and the two flight attendants he might have been, literally, pulverized.

Fortunately, his robust and influential Cousin Joe was also awaiting his arrival at the gate and, by enlisting the aid of a couple of policemen amongst the contingent there to detain the Snake Woman—as she was, henceforth, to be dubbed by the media—Herk was spirited away to the crew's quarters to await the arrival of his luggage, but not before he had taken an emotional leave of his confederate throughout this strange ordeal, Mr. Ed Williams. Herk hugged the older man and proffered his lasting appreciation for the support, while Willams, on his side, remarked to Cousin Joe on the skill and acumen of his new charge.

"That weapon was put to good use," Williams remarked and, as an addendum, concluded, "perhaps for the first time in its long existence."

While awaiting his luggage Herk was treated with considerable deference by the airline employees. They supplied him and Cousin Joe with coffee and soft drinks and, presently, delivered his luggage to the sequestered room in which they waited.

During his wait Herk proceeded to the bathroom with his sword where he inspected it and cleaned the blade of any remnants of the snake's blood. As he and Cousin Joe proceeded from the quarters, upon arrival of his luggage, one of the young ladies in employ of the airline said, gazing at the saber and with a giggle, "Good work! All men should have blades that effective."

Herkimer, in his country boy innocence, did not grasp the humor in this remark until he and Cousin Joe were ensconced in a taxi and heading out of the LaGuardia passage onto the expressway.

Cousin Joe was a tall man, narrow at the hips, his face a near perfect rectangle. His jaw protruded and his eyes gave forth a radiance of surety when he spoke.

"Well," he said with a bit of irony, "you certainly made a dramatic entrance into the Big Apple."

Herkimer took this as mild criticism. "I'm sorry," he said.

"Sorry! Why you saved a lot of people a lot of real trouble. You may have even saved some lives."

"I just did what I thought I had to do."

"My boy," said Joe in a parental mood, "I think you are just the kind of citizen this city needs." And he reached across and patted Herk on the thigh, being careful to avoid the sword which was standing between the younger male's knees. "But tell me," he continued, "why did you feel you had to carry that weapon with you?"

"My Grandfather Hampton gave it to me before he passed on," Herk said softly. "His father carried it in the Civil War. He told me to guard it for the rest of my life."

"I'm surprised they let you carry it on the plane."

Herk then told him of the difficulties he'd encountered and how the kindly Mr. Williams had come to his assistance.

"Well, they're certainly glad that they let you carry it aboard."

"Yeah," said Herk, perking up now, "you heard that lady as we left. She said all men should have blades so effective."

Cousin Joe had a hearty laugh from this. "I don't believe she meant one you carry in your hand but one that hangs between your legs."

For a moment the wit of the woman's remark still did not register with Herk but suddenly he raised his eyebrows and his face flushed. "Oh!" His mother had not permitted off-color jokes before her or when any woman was present, but when Herk saw the humorous intent of the woman's remark he gave his cousin a smile.

There was a tight back-up of cars at the broad bridge going across to Manhattan and Cousin Joe, sensing the diffidence of his new charge, made an attempt at further communication.

"How's your father—I guess I should say His Honor—the judge?"

"He's just fine. I saw him before I left."

"I take it you don't see him often."

"No. That's why I'm here." But feeling he had trod forbidden turf Herk hastened to make it a question, "Isn't it?"

"I reckon so," Cousin Joe said, returning to the jargon of his country heritage with a broad smile. After a few moments he continued. "Judge Herkimer Wilson Hampton. It's hard for me to believe he's such an honorable fellow; the two of us were such rascals when we were growing up." Cousin Joe sat back and folded his arms in recollection. "Some time I'll tell you about our exploits." He became more serious. "Of course, they won't seem like much to you—compared to what kids do today. We were quite tame. Just little rascals, that's all. We never did any real harm." With this statement Cousin Joe settled deeper into the seat and looked satisfied. "No real harm," he repeated.

By now they had passed through the toll gates and were on the way down the ramp onto The Island.

"There it is, my boy," said the man, a note of pride in his voice as though he had personally devised the towers of glass and concrete which stretched before them. "Gotham, the one true land of opportunity."

To the country boy his first view of the metropolis looked rather more like a frightening hodgepodge of stone, steel and glass. As they passed from the drive into the area of habitation he found one large edifice abutted by another by another. No greenery until, at one corner, they passed a plot where stood one tree surrounded by a meager lawn of green circumscribed by a steel railing. Presently, they turned down a broad thoroughfare separated into two parts by a cement island and, shortly after, through a passage in the bricks into a paved court encompassed, once more, by bricks—the walls of a tall apartment building.

"Well, here we are Herkimer, your new home!" cried the exuberant Cousin Joe.

They were welcomed at the entrance to the building by a doorman in uniform who plucked Herkimer's luggage from the trunk of the taxi, escorted them into the building and deposited them in an elevator which then hoisted them to the eighth floor. There they entered directly into an elaborate foyer.

"Sylvia," Joseph called. "Wherefore art thou, Sylvia?":

A woman appeared, stepping into the foyer from a doorway alongside the elevator entrance, one of four which accessed the space. She was a slender lady with taut legs, a lengthy, oval face, sharp features, straight, fair hair clipped precisely at her jaw line—attractive in a severe way.

"Well," she said, her broad lips extending in a smile as she cast a querulous look at the sword in Herkimer's hand. "Is this our little Herkie?"

"The new prince of Park Avenue," said Joe, proudly presenting the timid lad with a sweep of his hand, "complete with trusty saber, a family treasure of several generations and savior of Flight 285."

Sylvia was puzzled. "And what do you mean by that?" she said.

This prompted her husband to recount the tale of how Herkimer and his trusty weapon had prevented a hijack attempt.

"Oh, my goodness," spoke the elegant Sylvia. "We have a real hero in our family." And she seized Herk around the shoulders and placed a moist and noisy kiss on his cheek.

During this repartee Herk had been rendered curious by the lady's enunciation; it was strange to his ear. Did all Eastern women speak this way? Then from deep in his subconscious memory he thought he recalled his father, some years previous, jesting at his Cousin Joe's marriage to "a Southern vixen." His father, a zealous liberal, had not approved his favorite cousin's marriage to this woman, and now he had, without warning, entrusted his son into her care.

"Herkie," a sobriquet he detested, managed a tolerant smile and stood awaiting instructions.

"Come," said Sylvia after an awkward moment during which it was clear she had expected her husband to acquaint the boy with his new lodgings. "See your room." And as she led him by the hand through the door from which she had appeared she added, "Angelina, our cleaning lady, made it impeccable for you."

They passed through a spacious living room, a bit over furnished but elegant, turned quickly to the left through another doorway into a brief hall, on one side of which was a door opening into a toilet and bath, and took three steps into a pleasant chamber, large enough for more than one person, with a double-sized bed abutting the wall which led from the hallway. There was a door to a closet at the far right behind the bathroom, a cabinet of drawers against the wall opposite, with a desk and chair next to it, and a double casement window looking out onto the court and the other wing of the building at the far wall. On the bed was a comforter adorned with large prints of flowers, yellow, pink and blue, and the walls were decorated with a paper which matched the comforter in colors but with much smaller flowers. It appeared quite an attractive abode—for a young woman.

"Here we are, sweet Herkie," warbled the genial lady. "Bring your things and unpack. We shall celebrate with dinner at Il Monello. I shall insist, even above Joseph's objections. Your heroism deserves a treat."

He tossed the sword on the multi-colored bed cover and turned toward whence he'd come, expecting to retrieve his luggage. But Cousin Joe had anticipated him and arrived with the two bags clutched in his hands.

Herkimer was speedy in stowing his few possessions in cabinet and closet. Then he stood a moment, sword in hand, gazing out into the apartment complex and above to the sky, fading now into twilight. This was truly a foreign realm but he felt an exhilaration; it seemed that a new energy was transmitted to his sixth sense. He might like this new life into which he had been cast.

Many things would be strange to him as he discovered in dining at the Italian restaurant. There were, on the menu, more than one item named spaghetti and others with such strange names as penne and fettucini. At the suggestion of Lady Wilson he ordered ternera, not wanting to contradict her, and because he felt the need of some weighty carbohydrate he asked for risotto which, they assured him, was an Italian form of rice, and thus was begun a lifelong passion for that delicacy of Northern Italian cuisine.

Being an observant chap and one wont to obey rules of deportment he made no faux pas in his initial sally into the heretofore unknown community of upward mobility in New York and, therefore, slept well when finally implanted in his bed of flowers. He did lie for several minutes in the dark, fully alert, gazing out the broad casement to the edge of the building's further annex and beyond to the sky.

Even this was not the firmament of his homeland for no stars were visible in the constant glow which, rather than expanding his purview, seemed to envelop the sky in a translucence which cloaked the natural essence of the heavens. He reached to the floor and retrieved his saber from beneath the bed where he had stowed it earlier and clutched it to his side, sole bond, now, to his past.

Thus slept young Herkimer, in peace and safety on this eve of a lifetime of prodigious labor in the sometimes evil, sometimes beneficent, world of the latter half of Twentieth Century America, a true hero if only for a day.

II

It was decided that Herkimer should be enrolled in the Horney Academy, a private institution not six blocks from the Wilson apartment. It is quite probable that this school was chosen for propinquity rather than profundity. It was also popular among the social coterie of Lady Wilson to whom the approbation of this clique seemed most desirable.

Being a woman without children she was delighted to tell her friends that her ward was a colleague to their offspring and, despite his slight stature, an attractive one. She expected that many of the daughters of her crowd would fall enamored of her "little Herkie." He did, indeed, become the center of more than normal attention among his classmates, his diffidence aside. They were especially impressed by his strength, speed of foot and quickness to learn difficult disciplines such as soccer to which he devoted his first fall with sufficient success that by the close of the season he was a regular starter on the varsity squad. In the spring his athletic proficiency secured him further honor; he became, in his first year, the leading batsman on the baseball team, and his determination to excel was rewarded with inclusion on the Scholastic Honor Roll.

When the time came that spring for vacation from the rigors of the classroom Cousin Joe made the unilateral decision that Herkimer should become indoctrinated in some form of trade. He found our youth employment with a friend who was franchisee to a number of shops, scattered about the City, which produced copies of letters, manuscripts and such, prepared packets for mailing, delivered them to the Postal Service and dispatched documents by FAX, all for individuals or small firms which did not operate these services in their own offices or have mail rooms for such functions. The shops, in fact, were named "The Mail Room." Herk was sent to work in a Mail Room branch at mid-town, on Forty-sixth Street.

He was taught to pack various items for their regular customers, to operate the copying equipment and FAX. He was thought too young to deal with customers across the counter. He reported, each day, to the manager at eight A.M.—to catch the crowd bound for their offices—and was on duty until six P.M.—to catch the same ones quitting their work places. He had one hour for lunch.

There were five employees at this branch: the manager, a man scarcely more than forty years of age, two women and a third male, all three older than Herk by about ten years. One of the women was assigned to instruct him in the eccentricities of the electronic equipment as well as the proper mode of packing the items which came across the counter for shipping. She was a lady as small as

Herkimer, comely though not awesomely so, with long dark tresses. Her most noteworthy feature was a pair of eyes, dark almost to opacity, rounded to the near perfect ovals of the outer lenses of binoculars to which they showed a surprising similarity. The gentle lass, mid-twenties at most, spoke with a pronounced Hispanic stress though her grasp of English and its grammar were more than acceptable. Her smile was shy and effacing and Herkimer liked her immediately. His attraction was scarcely libidinous until he stepped within range of her perfume. The whiff of lavender which wafted to his nostrils had an immediate effect: his groin tingled, his willy twitched. It made his indoctrination the more difficult. When she was explaining the intricate workings of a packing machine he listened with a bothersome obstruction where the legs of his trousers joined.

When she was across the room, however, he felt no particular allure. Her legs were slim and straight and her hips narrow, yet her luminous disposition and cordiality made his labors, even late into the work day, pleasing. She was just nice to be around.

The most hectic time of day was the hour past noon when many customers left items for packaging and dispatched messages by FAX on their way to lunch. This meant that the employee's lunch hour did not begin until one P.M. and they were forced to take alternate periods. Herk and Ruth—for that was the name his tutor had given—were assigned the period from two until three. Ruth had chosen this later hour for, as she attested, this was the normal time for lunch in Mexico, her place of origin. Instead of leaving the premises for one of the many small eateries—they could scarcely be called restaurants—on their block she chose to bring sandwiches she had prepared at home and seclude herself in the store room, amongst the reams of paper and boxes stored there, and read. Her literature, if it could be called that, was invariably chosen from among the authors of romantic novels popular in that decade, Danielle Steele, Barbara Taylor Bradford and others who had the talent to hold their non-feminist audience in a trance.

When Herkimer discovered her mid-afternoon habit he began to pack his own lunch in the Park Avenue kitchen and carry it, in a brown paper bag, out the door each morning to the disdain of his guardian, Cousin Sylvia.

"Must you go out with that awful brown bag each day?" she asked on the third day on which he left clutching the sack.

"It's my lunch," he said. "I got some ham and bread and made a sandwich."

The next morning she supplied him with an attaché case and informed him that this was the proper carrier for anything, "even so basic as food."

He arrived at the Mail Room branch to raised eyebrows.

"Well," said Harry Crum, the manager. "Ain't we swell! Look at our new executive."

Herk had felt, from the beginning, a hostility from Crum. He supposed it arose from his being imposed upon this Mail Room branch by the boss, Cousin

Joe's friend. He blushed properly and hurried to hide the case in the stock room behind a rack of boxes.

Harry Crum was, as has been stated, a man of forty something, of a height above six feet and the frame of a scarecrow. His hair stood forth in curls from his gaunt face. His eyes, close together on either side of a narrow nose, seemed not to carry any message from the brain behind, and his flaccid chin seemed, daily, from noon onward, tainted with a dusty growth of stubble. It appeared that he had a more than fatherly interest in Herk's young Mexican colleague, and while it had been he who assigned her as tutor the resentful Crum now seemed to hold a jealous animosity toward Herk. He watched the two workmates closely when Herk was receiving his training on the various machines and when they went into the stock room where Herk was to learn packing and wrapping he looked in on them periodically under the guise that he wanted Herk taught properly.

"How's it goin'?" he would say, trying to appear as pleasant as his rigid face would allow.

The frail lady, however, was nothing but entirely proper; indeed, she would recoil if, by chance, Herk's body brushed hers ever so slightly. He stayed at a safe distance on most occasions for he admitted now to himself that it was not simply her perfume which had an amatory effect on his libido. When they retired to the stockroom at two P.M. each day to gratify their hunger he took a seat some distance from her.

Now he began to detect, in the looks of Harry Crum, an interest in Ruth which had little to do with supervision. Herk's unnatural impulse toward protection of the female species, instilled by his sainted mother, prompted him to stay fairly close to Ruth, especially when the other two workers were absent and Crum might otherwise find her alone. Indeed, when Crum occasionally looked in upon them in the stockroom during their lunch Herk saw rage in the manager's eyes at the presence of another male, him, Herkimer Hartland Hampton. This prompted him to make certain that his little tutor was never alone.

Crum's revenge was to make a messenger of Herkimer. Whenever business people housed in nearby buildings received an item from another of the Mail Room branches, instead of waiting for the regular deliveryman Crum would post Herk abroad on the task. And so it was that Herk became involved in a bizarre incident which brought him notoriety once again.

It was a few minutes before two P.M. on a Wednesday afternoon. Herk was returning to the Mail Room from a delivery. As he approached the plate glass window which shielded the work space within from passers-by he was pervaded by a strong sentiment that, inside, something was amiss. Crum was standing behind the counter both hands laid upon the edge as though to hold himself erect. Across the counter stood a man as tall as Crum but much broader in a loose jacket with a baseball cap pulled far down on his skull; one hand was in a pocket of the jacket forcing the material forward in a bulge. Crum looked at the man in high apprehension while behind him Ruth stood at the cash register, one of their large mailing envelopes in her hand, doing what Herk could not discern. This happened in a moment and Herk darted back out of sight of anyone inside the shop.

He paused there only another moment, long enough to suck a deep lung full of air, then ran to the door, kicked it open and pounced on the hulk standing at the counter. The man cried out and attempted to turn but Herkimer had both hands on his neck in a stupefying clutch. The behemoth gave one weak cry, his knees collapsed and he fell sideways to the floor, his head, with help from Herkimer, broadcasting a sonorous "Bonk!" as it struck the marble surface. The brute lay silent as Herk swiftly probed his jacket pocket and extracted a pistol.

"Oh, my God! My God!" muttered Harry Crum before his knees gave out as he tried to stumble toward the passage through the counter.

"Herkie! Herkie!" cried Ruth as she scurried through the passage to his side and, kneeling, threw her arms about his shoulders. "Are you all right?"

"Quick!" said Herk, holding the pistol firmly against the intruder's temple. "Get me some rope."

She looked at him, her eyes a blank.

"Some cord. From the stock room."

She hurried back through the passage and into the stock room as Crum poked his head above the counter.

"Call the police," Herk ordered his boss, still holding the nasty weapon against the failed culprit.

Crum took up the telephone and was punching for the operator when Ruth came back through the passage and handed Herk a ball of twine.

By now the robber was conscious but the pistol to the head was an adequate deterrent. While Ruth held the gun to his head Herk rolled the bandit onto his belly and drew his hands together behind his back. Herk's Boy Scout training was, for the first time, truly appreciated for he was able to wrap and secure the man's wrists together tightly at the base of his spine.

Meantime, Crum was yelping into the telephone, "Police! Police! We've had a robbery, a robbery! But we caught the robber." Pause. "Yes. That's right, attempted robbery. We got him!"

Already, outside the window, a small throng had gathered to look in to where Herk and Ruth still knelt beside the prone hulk who was moaning loudly now.

Ruth stood beside Herk, looking down, at first in consternation but now in admiration. She was actually smiling at her young pupil and three minutes did not elapse before two policemen burst through the door.

Herk looked up at them and Ruth stood beaming behind him.

"What's goin' on here?" said one cop, looking down at the pistol which Herk still held.

"We caught the crook," said the suddenly brave Crum, stepping forward through the passage.

"Herkie did!" said Ruth with pride, looking down at her colleague kneeling beside the prostrate intruder.

Herk stood and presented the confused cop with the dark weapon.

"How in hell did you do that?" asked the second policeman.

"Like this," said Ruth and she put her hands gently around Herkimer's throat. "And then cast him to the piso."

"What?"

"I threw him down and he struck his head on the floor," said Herk.

The failed robber was beginning to move with more energy. He rolled as far to his side as his secured arms would allow but made no attempt to look at anyone. The first policeman looked down at the failed bandit, then at Herk and, finally, to Ruth.

"Come on! Yuh tryin' ta tell me dis kid dropped dat big guy?"

"Yes," said Ruth in delight.

"Well, Sir," said Herkimer, "I got him from behind. I surprised him."

"You must be awful strong to get that bugger down."

"Well, Sir, I got him by the neck and squeezed. He passed out and fell down. I just helped him. And anyway ... sir ... I am kind of strong. I lift weights."

"Oh, I see..." the cop was unconvinced.

"Hey, Mike," said his partner, stepping forward and squeezing Herk's biceps between his thumb and forefinger, "duh kid's powerful. I kin see dat. Can't youse?"

With that they turned their interest to the man on the floor. Each cop took him by an armpit and lifted him to his feet.

"Come on, Creep," said the one named Mike.

The big, would-be robber, whose head stood some inches above even the taller policeman, fell against him, still quite unsteady.

Before turning toward the door the cop called Mike said, "One a ya's gonna hafta come wit us." He looked to Ruth. "Why don't youse come. Yuh seem ta know how it happened."

"We all know, officer," said Crum stepping forward through the passageway. "It was me who called you."

"Nobody called us. Some guy on duh street stopped us. Said dere was some trouble in heyuh," said Mike.

It was at this precise instant that a police car pulled to a halt in the street, blocking traffic so that it was soon backed up through the Fifth Avenue crossway. A tall officer, his tunic shining in brass, stepped from the vehicle and, scattering the assemblage on the sidewalk with shoves and lurches, forced his way through and into the shop.

"Glad to see you're already here, Sergeant," said the newly arrived officer. "We got a call that there was a hold-up."

"We stopped 'em," said Crum boldly. "And I called you."

"Herkie stopped them! Oh, it was so exciting!" put in Ruth, sparkling with enthusiasm.

"Who's Herkie?" asked the Captain, for the two bars on his collar signaled his rank as that.

"Herkimer," said our young man, stepping forward a pace.

"Well, let's get him outa here," said the Captain. "We got traffic tied up out there."

The rabble had expanded into the street and across it. No cars could pass.

Over the weak protest of Crum, who complained that he could not work alone, the police took both Herkimer and Ruth with them.

"The others will be back from lunch soon," chirped Ruth, and they were conveyed through the crowd and into the patrol car while the sergeant and his partner escorted the stumbling brigand to their vehicle which was parked alongside the curb.

"What happened? What's going on?" came crows from the crowd, but the glum officers paid them no mind. Ruth, however, responded cheerfully, "Herkie stopped el ladron."

At the precinct Herk told his story, how he was returning from a delivery when he discovered the man across the counter from Crum and that he never thought of doing anything different from what he did. Ruth, of course, embellished his account with recollections of her own: how the big guy had strode into the shop when the others had left for lunch and she and Crum were the only ones present. More than anything she seemed intent on establishing Herk's heroism as she described the manner in which he seized the large man's neck and threw him to el piso with a ringing thump.

The captive was silent through all, gazing vaguely across the room, still obviously bemused. He did not look so much a dangerous thug as he did an inoffensive imbecile. His face was more than half jaw and chin and he seemed not to notice anyone about him. His hands remained tied at his back as Herk had secured them. The police officers made no move to either untie them or replace the rope with handcuffs.

Sitting alongside the railing which separated the lobby of the precinct from the sanctum of cells in back was a man with a pad of paper and pencil writing vigorously as Herk and Ruth told of their adventure and when they were excused he accosted them.

"Please," he said, "can we talk. I'm from **The Daily News**."

Herk had never read anything from **The News**. **The Times and Wall Street Journal** were the only periodicals allowed in Cousin Joe's abode, but Ruth was ecstatic.

"Oh, yes," she said. "Herkie, we'll be in the newspaper."

And indeed they were—in not just one but all the newspapers, for they were met outside the precinct house by more reporters, each with a photographer. They were front page in the tabloids while **The Times** and **Newsday** relegated the tale to the local sections.

"*Youth Subdues Desperado*," hailed **The News** while **The Post** was a bit more imaginative and personal: "*Herkie Foils Felon—Again!*" For **The Post** reporter had been more thorough and discovered that it was, indeed, the same young man who had thwarted the hi-jacker a year previous. Alongside the forty point type in the tabloids was a picture of Herkimer with Ruth at his side, her arm about his shoulders, her other hand holding proudly to his near one, presenting her hero to the heretofore unsuspecting townspeople.

"Who is that woman?" cried cousin Sylvia when she saw the picture—it seems the doorman had slipped her a copy of **The Post**—thrusting the newsprint beneath Herkimer's eyes.

Herk answered in a manner he thought would assuage her choler.

"She's my teacher at the shop," he said. "She made it possible for me to work properly."

"And what is she teaching you?" Sylvia said with a cynical snarl.

Herk did not grasp the nasty entendre. "She taught me to use my tools."

"Oh, my God!" cried Sylvia, missing the plural ending on the, to her, salacious object. "We shall discuss this with Joseph when he returns from Washington tomorrow."

So Herkimer was hero only outside the walls of Apartment 42 at 1191 Park Avenue. The inhabitants of the other apartments in the complex, however, seemed pleased to have the young celebrity beneath their roof. The doorman met him with an effusive smile when he left the building for work next day.

"I guess you showed them crooks what's up, Mr. Herkimer."

"There was only one, Charley," said the modest lad. "But it was kind of scary. I think I'll go and learn karate somewhere."

"Good idea," said Charley. "Everyone in this city oughta learn karate. Maybe that'ud stop some a the crime."

"Do you know karate, Charley?"

"Naw, I'm too old for that."

"No you're not, Charley. You're never too old to learn how to protect yourself."

"You think so?"

"I know so. Maybe we can find a good school and go together," said Herk as he strolled, jaunty and confident onto the Avenue.

But he was to discover that his life had acquired complexity. As he scuttled over to Fifth Avenue to catch the bus downtown people stared at him when he paused at the crossings. As he boarded the bus the driver looked at him closely, and when he moved down the aisle toward the back of the bus eyes turned to follow his progress. When he sat in the row of seats at the far back a young woman leaned across the person between and, with amusement in her expression, asked him directly, "Aren't you the fellow who stopped the robbery?"

The modest Herkimer smiled and nodded.

The activity at The Mail Room branch was frenzied. From opening to closing, the small room was thronged with curious people who wished to see "where the fellow caught the robber." Crum was not pleased as most of the visitors requested an audience with "that kid who caught him." He asserted that attention was being diverted from their business. But it appeared, at the end of the day, that business had not been adversely affected for it proved to be a banner day for this branch. They had the largest cash return of all locations in the city. This took much puff from the chest of the envious Crum, who at one time during the day had muttered to one of the other employees that he would "get that little bastard fired or transferred."

It was scarcely necessary for Crum to react so, for Cousin Sylvia came to his aid. "You shall work no longer in the same environs with that slut," she informed Herk upon his arrival at the apartment that evening.

"What?" Herk was astonished; he knew not what she meant.

"You will not be permitted to work with that lascivious woman. Your *tutor*, as you euphemistically describe her."

"Ruth? Nothing is wrong with Ruth. She's a sweet lady." Herkimer was angry now. The bristling Sylvia did not yet know that it was hazardous to pique his ire. Herk had a retentive character. He was unlikely to forget this slur on one he so admired.

"Yes, she's sweet all right. I know her type by sight. She'll sweeten up to you and seduce you."

Cousin Sylvia was of stern southern stock. Born to an affluent doctor in Durham she was schooled in proper academies and colleges for young ladies of the Fifties. She had matriculated at Wellesley College and upon graduation had married Joseph Wilson whom she had met while he was studying the ways of commerce at Harvard Business School and whose vitality and acuity were already in evidence. She was a disciple of a popular radio evangelist and considered herself a Christian of morals above challenge. She was determined that Herkimer should not consort with one so beneath him in the social order.

Herk accepted, with equanimity, his sentence. He had been given, by his father, as ward to his cousin and wife and he would never consider a challenge to his father's will. Yet his outward composure belied the nauseating resentment which, now, he felt in his mid-section. When Cousin Joe returned that evening from his business trip they held a three way conference, for which Herkimer was grateful; some part of his anger was relieved. Cousin Joe was pleased when shown the front page of THE POST, an act which Sylvia performed to impress upon him the danger to their ward in holding positions in "lower class" places of employment. Joe did not seem disconcerted by the photo of Herk and "that social climbing bitch" but did acquiesce to his wife's demand that their young charge should find employment in more genteel surroundings and for the remainder of that vacation period Herk served in a different mail room, that of Cousin Joe's firm.

His celebrity followed him there and even back to school that Fall. For him it seemed a burden, but later, in looking back on that last year of high school, he saw that it had, in some respects at least, enhanced his experience: the young ladies were attracted to him as never previously and even the athletic coaches looked upon him with a new regard.

III

It was during this, his final year in the Horney School, that Herkimer decided to follow Charley the doorman's suggestion and so found a Tae Kwon Do school where he might learn and practice the art of Karate. He even convinced his cousin Joe of the advantage to the apartment complex if their doorman were a practiced Black Belt Karate to the extent that Joe agreed to advance the necessary funds that Charley might accompany Herk in his search for security of self and property. The two of them went off together on Monday, Wednesday and Friday evenings to practice the martial art of Nippon. This training proved to be of more value than a mere feeding of vanity. Not long after they had completed the first stage of their training, late on a dark night when Charley was drowsing in his guard room at the entrance to the apartment complex he was shocked awake by a piercing scream from somewhere on Park Avenue. In curiosity he went out onto the sidewalk and looked for the origin of the sound. He was rewarded with the sight, just at the downtown corner, of what appeared to be a woman with two dark figures assaulting her. The Avenue was barren of other activity.

Without hesitation Charley hurried toward the scene where the crime was being enacted. As he drew near he saw that it was, indeed, two men who had grappled a woman to now helpless subjection. One was behind encircling her neck with his arm, his opposite hand covering her mouth; the other was before her, trousers fallen to his ankles, preparing to take his pleasure.

"Stop!" cried Charley.

The assailants looked to see a slight, aging man in livery scurrying rapidly down the sidewalk. The scoundrel facing the woman turned, his assault weapon projecting stiff before him.

"Ged ouda here, old man," he snarled. And bending over to his fallen trousers retrieved a dark object from which he clicked a lengthy blade.

Charley advanced undaunted, which prompted the rapist to draw up and fasten his trousers, then step toward the doorman and make a sweeping slash aimed at Charley's neck. Our Black Belt was not intimidated but with agility avoided the blade, seized the thug by the wrist and, with one snappy turn, threw the culprit to the cement. The man hastened to arise but a swift chop from Charley's hand to the Adam's apple and a sharp toe to the gonads rendered the felon inert, senseless on the street.

The second criminal was now forced to release his hostage and face the raging nemesis. The woman dashed away and disappeared before Charley could complete the rout by disposing of the second knave as he had the first.

Charley quickly removed the shoelaces from the feet of the half-conscious brutes, tied their hands behind their spines and their ankles together much as

Herk had secured The Mail Room miscreant, then dashed to the apartment complex and dialed the police from the phone in his doorman chambers. The men in blue were there in a trice and the malefactors were hastened away to the precinct.

Some occupants of the building who had taken notice of the ruckus in the street descended to join the doorman and were able to affirm, to the police, the validity of his story. One had heard the woman's cry and peered from the windows above to observe the confrontation. Though the newspapers carried no report of the incident, all in the immediate environs soon knew of the doorman's intrepidity, especially those in 1191 Park which thereafter carried the nom de guerre "Hero House," sheltering the two known redeemers of the neighborhood.

While Herk and Charley studied Karate, Herk also availed himself of the weight room at the Tae Kwon Do school and the combination of weights and Karate was to prove of great benefit.

By the spring of his final year in Horney School he had secured a position as short stop on the baseball team. He was extremely quick and adept at darting right or left to prevent ground balls from reaching the field behind him. He also proved clever as well as proficient with the bat. He struck the ball frequently and with potency but he was especially good at waiting out the opposing mounds men. His compact size made it difficult for pitchers to place the ball within the valid striking zone. He was awarded more bases on balls than the remainder of his teammates together and it became a near certainty that he would score a run at least once, more often twice, in each contest.

Upon occasion the Horney Hornets—for that was the mascot chosen for them decades previous—would tour the provinces, trekking to Westchester County to engage the hardball nines of schools located there. Often, they would play one team on a Friday early evening and another Saturday morning, spending the night on cots in one of the rival gymnasiums. It was on one such itinerary that a particularly odious incident occurred.

Fresh from a triumph over the minions of Hackley School they arrived, across the county, at Rye Country Day where, next morning, they were to engage that institution's finest. They were shown to a corner of the gym where mats had been laid for them. After a hasty repast of ham sandwiches, cola and chocolate bars, served in the school's cafeteria they repaired to their quarters, weary and eager for repose. It was then that an odor, odd but somehow familiar to Herk, was perceived.

They prepared to retire but the scent not only persisted it grew more potent to the point that it became clear their chance of slumber would be seriously inhibited.

Could it be, they wondered, that this was a prank perpetrated by their opponents with the purpose to render them sleepless and therefore feeble for their encounter the following day? Their coach, Ben Rorty, believed there was no harmful intent but that the caretaker had merely neglected to clean the premises adequately. But upon careful inspection of the large hall it was discovered by our painstaking investigator, Herkimer, and two of his comrades that the space beneath the radiators which surrounded the room were engorged with pecks and pounds of feces; whether human, animal or a combination did not much matter for whatever the origin the room was rife with a pungency growing more virile each moment until the stench had become sickening.

When Herk and friends reported their discovery Mr. Rorty was seized with a choler which caused his face to flush brightly, the tendons of his neck to bulge and his speech to become profane.

"Good damn those bastards," he snarled to his assistant, George Walsh, "they have fucked up this room purposely. Well, we'll fuck them right back." He stomped toward the door. "Come on." He waved to the group. "We'll leave 'em without any opponent. See how they like that!"

But the intrepid Herkimer hurried to the door and approached the seething coach.

"Excuse me, Sir," he said, "but that is just what they want. Then we'll forfeit and we're in first place in the league."

"Christ man!" scowled Rorty, "we can't live with this stench. We'll all be sick. We won't be able to play well, if at all."

"Excuse me, Sir, but I saw some buckets in a room over in that corner when we came in. We can put the crap in them and throw it outside."

Rorty looked at Herk as though the younger man were mouthing nonsense, but then his face split in a broad grin and his eyes expanded.

"We'll throw it right on the steps to their locker room," Rorty exclaimed.

Herkimer's early training in the barnyards of Iowa had instilled a will to solve practical problems and manure was to him simply another object to be dealt with. Enlisting the aid of several other players he directed a clean-up. They moved the sleeping mats to the center of the room; they found the buckets and brooms in what was apparently the caretaker's closet; they swept the feces from beneath the radiators and down the floor to a place before the exit where it made a rather expansive, redolent heap. Then, placing the sides of the buckets to the floor, they swept them full of excrement, took them outside and around the building to the door to the locker room and there deposited the contents. After five such trips the floor, while stained with the remains was, nonetheless, free of the large mass of shit.

Still the scraps and scrapes on the floor and beneath the radiators gave off an unhealthy fragrance and their task seemed a failure until the enterprising Herkimer appeared in the doorway to the closet brandishing the operative end of a rubber hose.

"Now, boys," he whooped, "if some of you will grab brooms and someone will hold open the doors we'll turn on this hose and give the floor a good dowsing."

The others joined him, those not pushing brooms or holding doors shouting encouragement in strident chant, "Go men go! Go men go!" Within a quarter of an hour the floor was clean all around, and the gymnasium once more habitable. There remained a faint odor but nothing so strong that it would prevent sleep.

Before retiring Coach Rorty addressed the group: "Men," he said with solemnity, "I'm proud to be your coach. We will sleep well, now, and in the morning we will go out there and beat the crap out of these damned Country Dayers." He raised his arm above his head and the gang all roared.

"One last thing," he added. "We owe a great thanks to Herk Hampton who showed us that it pays to have a country boy around."

Once more they cheered and those near Herk smacked him about the shoulders in congratulatory enthusiasm.

Next morning, after arising and enjoying an invigorating shower the team, as a unit, was making its way to the cafeteria led by Mr. Rorty and his assistant when the two of them were approached by a tall, thin man in spectacles who appeared to be an official of the hosting school. This man called the two Horneyites aside and engaged them in trenchant discourse. The boys did not hear what the Country Day man said but they could see he was highly exercised and heard clearly the reply of their coach.

"Listen, you creep," bellowed Rorty, "someone from your place stuffed crap all around our sleeping quarters. I mean shit, man. It would've stunk us out, but damned if we are going to forfeit this game. We cleaned your Goddam gym for you. You should thank us for that! What do you think—we brought all that shit with us on the bus? Think, man, think!" And he stomped away, waving his team to follow, leaving the Country Day man astounded, mute.

The baseball contest in which they engaged some two hours later could scarcely be called that. It was no contest but a rout. Six Horney players, including Herk, hit home runs; they made four double-plays including one accomplished single handed by Herk when he snared a liner and stepped on second base to retire both the batter and runner, the only Country Day player to reach so far as second during the whole of the seven innings played. The tote in the end showed fourteen for Horney and zero for Country Day. It did appear that the host members played with less than fervor as though, perhaps, they had been a bit chastened.

This was the high point of the Horney baseball season yet they did continue to win. They ended the season with fourteen victories and only two defeats both coming the same weekend during which Herkimer and several of his team mates suffered from rotten spring colds and were not able to perform at the peak of their powers. Nonetheless the Horneyites were presented a giant trophy, memorial to their honor as champions of the Manhattan-Westchester Private League, commonly referred to as the Manchester League. Herk, along with two other Senior Class members of the squad were appointed to receive the trophy from the head mistress of Horney before an assemblage of all students in the school auditorium. During this ceremony it was announced that Herkimer Hartland Hampton had been named Most Valuable Player by the league's committee of coaches, this for his batting average of .430 and his nine home runs.

Herk was duly proud but typically diffident. "There are a lot of guys on this team who deserve it more than I. I was just lucky," he said when presented with the scroll which proclaimed him Most Valuable.

He was to stride the boards of the auditorium stage once more that spring to deliver the valedictory address at the graduation exercises. At this he was not nearly so humble. While he spoke of *"we"*, meaning his classmates, it seemed to the parents who crowded the hall that he was speaking at them as oracle of the new generation. He was, in actuality, espousing the ethics and social mores of a previous generation, the Arcadian culture of his parents and grandparents, with a bit of top-spin from the idealism of the generation just previous to his.

"We will go from here and on to a better world which we will help to define and to re-build. A world in which honesty is once more the primary virtue. Where a person's word is his or her bond, where cheating and lying will see a person ostracized from civil society, where accumulation of material things—money—will no longer be the standard by which we are judged and our community relations will be characterized by respect for others and a willingness to listen to them even when we disagree with their point-of-view. A world in which the color of peoples' skin, hair, eyes, the shape of their face, the language spoken, will have no bearing on the compassion we feel for them in our hearts. We will in our lifetime perhaps not see a simple global community but will nonetheless see a world where absolute tolerance is the rule and not the exception. Is this too much to expect? We surely hope not, for our generation will work for just such a world."

With this he folded the paper from which he read, marched from the stage, down steps to the orchestra where he took a seat among his peers. This action. being so abrupt and following such a proclamation from a teenager, left the audience, for the moment, stupefied, silent. But as he took his seat one bold listener behind him made a quiet slapping sound with his hands. This was reinforced by a similar act of another hardy soul and soon the audience was responding with tumultuous applause.

It was with difficulty that Ms. Klaus, head mistress of Horney, who marched to the podium next, managed to quiet the response so that she might be heard.

"Thank you," she broadcast; and again more resolutely, "Thank you!" And after a moment, when the crowd became settled, "I'll bet you didn't expect to hear such an oration from one so young. We are all proud of Herkimer, but that's what we've come to expect from our students here at Horney."

It was thus Herk concluded his days at The Horney School.

IV

In the Fall Herk was to matriculate at Occom College, a school in the upper reaches of New England with a reputation for both scholastic achievement and a raucous undergraduate social life. Cousin Joe had envisioned for Herkimer an education at Yale.

Herk had a 750 score on his SAT tests and Joe had done the proper networking to assure his nephew admission at New Haven, but the self-willed country boy had been particularly impressed by the arrogance of all those with whom he had contact in the admission process at Old Eli's institution and stood firm against his guardian, choosing, instead the more relaxed attitude of the Occom administrators.

While passing time awaiting the Fall term, Herk toiled in the Big Apple Orchard as a clerk in the mail room of a Wall Street firm headed by Cousin Joe's friend, J.C. Kashin, where he would learn, first hand, the encompassing power of manipulation and the need to suspend the temptation to question the wisdom of prevailing dogma if one were to progress through the labyrinth of "advancement."

During the first month of employment a middle aged employee of the firm, Kashin, Marker & Foxx, discovered, in some mysterious manner, that their youngest clerk was to matriculate in September at Occom College. The fellow, whose name was Leonard Hedburgh, approached young Hampton and announced that he had heard Herk was headed for Occom and that he, Hedburgh, was an alumnus of that very institution.

"I'm excited about going there," Herk said looking upward, for Hedburgh was several hands higher than the younger man, thin to the point of a positive display of bones along his arm when his shirt sleeves were drawn back, as now they were.

"I'm sure you'll love it," Hedburgh said. His angular jaw seemed to move extravagantly when he spoke. "Of course it's not the same as when I went there. They've started to let in girls."

"Yes," said Herkimer with propriety, "I don't believe I'd go there if they didn't."

"Oh, my boy, it was so wonderful back then. So virile. So... macho!" Hedburgh's eyebrows descended on his bony sockets.

"Macho? What's that?"

"Mexican expression, I believe. It means a guy who's really...well, tough, manly."

"Oh," Herk responded quietly, gazing up at this man who looked as though he might hardly endure a vigorous game of tag. "They told me they were known for intellectual pursuits."

"Well," said Hedburgh, a note of condescension in his voice. "Old Occom can certainly give you that. I suppose the girls won't hold you back much." He patted Herk on the shoulder and vanished from the mail room.

This left Herk a bit pensive. Perhaps all these Eastern schools were filled with stuffy guys. Maybe he should have gone back to the University in Iowa City. But Cousin Joe, and even his father, had urged upon him an Eastern education. Cousin Joe had gone to the University of Virginia and then to business school at Harvard. His father, as well situated as he was, yet held up his cousin Joe as an example of what one could do to advance himself in life with the proper education.

Hedburgh, however, proved himself, through the weeks, a cheery fellow and Herk came to appreciate him. He loved to spew short jokes and one-line quips at his colleagues and often used Herk to audition one before circulating it in the organization. These were usually indecorous and likely to be chauvinistically biased, and Herkimer, being inclined to adulate women, because of his strong attachment to the memory of his mother, most often did not appreciate them. In fact, he often did not even understand the supposed humor. But Hedburgh proved thoughtful of Herk's well-being and they did bond a certain friendship. This concord led to an event of good fortune which Herk was to effect to the enrichment of Hedburgh, and Cousin Joe.

Kashin, Marker & Foxx was a firm which, though dealing primarily in the purchase and sale of stocks and bonds, had an investment banking arm as well as a small department which dealt in commodities futures. This last department consisted of Leonard Hedburgh, who managed it, and a few other traders.

Cousin Joe had urged Herkimer to be alert and learn all he could of the investment business, that it would be of value in whatever trade he finally chose to pursue. In fact, the machinations of the market did fascinate him. He was particularly enthralled by the idea of "Puts" and "Calls" on margin where one need spend no actual cash and still make money if he were smart—and lucky. This interest led him also to investigate Hedburgh's field of commodities futures. It had the scent of the farm about it, back to his roots. He could fairly sniff the rancid effluvium of the barnyard when he saw the quote for "pork bellies" on the screen of Hedburgh's computer.

For Hedburgh had truly befriended the young man, had schooled him in the mysteries of the PC and welcomed him into the world of high-stakes gambling. Herk was now able, at any given moment, to click up the current quotes on anything in the market, commodity or stock. Since his father still raised pigs on his farm in Southern Iowa, pork bellies exerted a call to his attention. While being instilled with many of the ancient virtues which seemed anathema to his generation, Herk was yet a child of his times. He could not resist the PC and since Hedburgh was so generous as to allow him free access at lunch time one could usually discover Herkimer seated at the feet of Earth's latest sovereign, wafting from URL to URL, no one having the power to secure his attention for more than a minute or two until one day he happened, by accident, to click up a page of futures quotes. He was about to click to the next location when the designation "pork bellies" arrested his attention. He had skimmed past them a couple of times in his wanderings and the second time he thought that, if he recalled correctly, the quotes had been lower than the first. This triggered in him recall of a conversation he'd had recently with his father. He still telephoned the Judge a couple of times a month to report on his condition. In his most recent contact, not more than two days previous, the Judge had told him that they had, only the day before, discovered a disease in one swine of the herd which seemed to be disseminating rapidly for it was, that morning, discovered in three more. They had separated the four from the rest but did not believe they had taken the steps soon enough. They were fearful lest they lose the entire drove. Could it not happen that this blight might spread to affect pigs all across Iowa, the heart of the region with the largest population of swine in all the world? And if this should, indeed, occur would it not, then, raise the price of pork bellies to untoward heights?

Herkimer did not fancy the idea of taking advantage of others' bad fortune to bulge the bellies of already wealthy sharks, but he was, after all, in the employ of one such school of creatures and owed it to those who paid his wages to do the best he could to earn them. Besides he had an uncontrollable urge to prove himself as more than a clerk. It would be an adventure, and in the end, if his conjecture proved wrong no one would be hurt beyond reparation.

He decided he must inform Hedburgh of his discovery but, first, he would inform his father of action the Judge might take to alleviate the loss he must certainly take on his swine herd.

"Father," he said when the Judge had answered his telephone call, "how are your pigs?"

"I'm afraid we'll lose most of them, Son."

"And will this sickness spread to other farms?"

"It already has. I'm afraid this will be a bad year for pig farmers."

"I think I have a way you can avoid the loss on yours."

The Judge had infinite faith in the intelligence of his son but not necessarily in his judgment. Herk had, after all, only recently attained the age of eighteen.

"Now Son..." the Judge began to remonstrate.

"No, Dad, listen: if most of the pigs die then the price of the meat from those few left will go up—very high. If you would just find someone in Des Moines who trades in commodities futures you could put some money on pork bellies and sell them when the price skyrockets on the news of this pig blight."

When Herk told Hedburgh of his insider information the older man's eyes took on a glaze and stood in silence for several seconds, staring past his informant and then, slowly, his lips began to twitch and he smiled. Finally he spoke, a note of jubilation in his voice.

"Herkimer, my boy, do you realize what you are doing? You are going to make me the number one trader in commodities for this year." And off he scampered to deliver the news to his bosses. He would tip the scales of the market with the weight of his trades, primarily for himself and his bosses, which created a small crisis at Kashin, Marker and Fox. They could not let everyone in the firm profit; they might then be charged and prosecuted for insider trading. Never mind that most business was contracted on this quite simple premise, when the entire market suffered someone harmed by the shift might decide to call in a chip owed him by some judge somewhere. No, they must proceed cautiously. Only the partners named on the stationery masthead and Mr. Hedburgh would be allowed to suckle the pig fat. It was not more than twenty minutes after Herk's revelation that Hedburgh called him into his private domain for a chat.

"Now, Herkimer," said Hedburgh with serious demean, "you are a very smart young man..."

"Thank you Sir."

"...and I know you would not want to cause any...uh, catastrophe in our market."

"Oh no, Sir."

"Have you...told anyone else this information you gave me about the...uh...futures market and pork bellies?"

"Well, Sir, I did talk to my father about it, but he didn't even seem interested."

"And your father—what does he do?"

"He's a judge, Sir on the Supreme Court in Iowa. Well, actually, he's the Chief Justice."

Hedburgh's countenance, no longer complaisant, took on an air of terror. His eyebrows arched.

"And what did you ... did you discuss the possible repercussions of his news?"

"I just told him to buy some futures on pork bellies. I don't think he even knew what I meant, so I told him to get some broker in Des Moines to buy some for him."

"Oh, my God!"

"Did I do something wrong, Sir?"

Hedburgh's face relaxed and he shook his head in resignation. "My boy," he said in a condescending tone, "we are in a special situation here. It is our duty to protect the interests of our clients. Please don't tell anyone else. We might be accused of insider trading." He gave emphasis to the word insider, promptly dismissed Herkimer and scurried off to sell pork bellies on the futures.

As transpired, of course, Hedburgh and his superiors, Messieurs Kashin, Marker and Foxx, when they cashed in a month hence, profited by perhaps a million dollars apiece as did a few of Hedburgh's choice clients.

Herk was disappointed to learn that Judge Hampton had not acted on his advise but decided that, in the end, his conscience was more clear than it might have been had the Judge profited heavily.

There was, in addition, an odd effect to our young friend's discovery which illustrates the bizarre nature of the money-changing business. Leonard Hedburgh had one cunning rival for advancement at KMF. His name was Carl Manipol. Herk had more than once interrupted Manipol poaching on Hedburgh's files, hoping to gain, Herk supposed, some advantage in their competition for preference.

During the procedure on pork bellies Herk, one evening when he had stayed late to tidy his small corner of the message center, spied Manipol stealing his way into Hedburgh's office and closing the door. Manipol had not noticed Herk and so the intrepid mail room clerk, after making certain that they were the only employees still at work, crept down the hall to peep through the key slot. He was rewarded by a clear angle at Hedburgh's desk and particularly his computer. There, he observed, with indignation, the malevolent Manipol study the screen, then click several keys. He watched the thieving cur click several more times then burst into a wicked grin. "Ha!" Herk heard him cry and then watched him rub his hands together voluptuously.

Manipol clicked the keyboard several times more, then slapped his hands together and exclaimed something Herk did not hear clearly. Manipol made a few more entries, then began to shut down the computer and Herk scurried quietly to the message center to await the rogue's departure.

He waited for perhaps half an hour, until all lights save those in the outer hall were dark, and then crept once more to Hedburgh's office. He slithered inside and noiselessly closed the door, found the light switch and brightened the room once again. He turned on the computer and in a very short time had found what he had suspected to be true. Manipol had insinuated his way into the document prepared for ordering the "futures" sale of the commodity in question. There, thanks to his previous investigations into the operations of Hedburgh's department, Herk was able to discern that Manipol had included himself as a seller. The young clerk quickly changed Manipol from seller to buyer and on the morrow, when the transactions were processed it was discovered that Manipol had been rendered bankrupt. In fact, late in the morning, as he was passing Hedburgh's office, Herk looked in the open door to see a pallid Manipol facing Hedburgh who was quietly pronouncing, "You're dead Manipol. No one in this town will hire you. I'll see to that! I suggest you, perhaps, move to California. Or maybe Hong Kong."

You would surmise, perhaps, that Kashin, Marker & Foxx would reward their youthful conqueror of the pigs, with special treatment at the least. The opposite was their response. Hedburgh contrived to ignore him, to act as though he were an invisible servant, until two days after they had called in their futures. Herkimer was then informed that his presence in the mail room was no longer required. He was dismissed.

"We can't have such an inexperienced fellow giving tips around here," Hedburgh told him.

There was, however, one other investor who made money on the pork belly fiasco that year. When Herk learned the plan was to sell rather than buy he advised his Cousin Joe, warning him of the possible consequences of a too open secret. The process seemed no mystery to Cousin Joe who managed to garner a few hundred thousand in a transaction he made through another Wall Street friend. So Herkimer was a hero of sorts in the eyes of Joe and the trader through whom Joe dealt, for that hearty soul also profited greatly.

V

Two months remained before Herk must matriculate at Occom College and Cousin Sylvia was determined that he not spend the time idling in the apartment. She found him employment through a friend who was a buyer at Bloomingdale's Department Store. He became stock clerk for the women's accessories department.

It was a rather boring job which consisted mainly of finding the proper storage shelves for the merchandise when delivered from the supplier and helping the women salespeople to find, unpack and refill empty display racks and cases.

The storage room for women's accessories was a dark recess entered through a narrow passage which opened behind the floor-length mirrors where ladies could investigate the improvement, or lack of it, certain accessories might make to their image.

There was one chair on which Herk was to post himself awaiting the calls from the salespeople for more items or from the floor manager urging him to report at the dock and assist in the unloading of a truck packed with dry goods. During the interim between calls for assistance Herk had taken to reading while perched on his chair, straining his eyes to decipher the type in the shadowy light from the lamp above his head, one of only two in the space. In truth, it was so obscure he found it necessary to ask his supervisor for a flashlight so that he might more quickly deliver the goods from storage when requested. Each shelf of items had on it a small tag specifying the nature of the merchandise hidden there. And hidden it was, for in the gloom it was nearly impossible to read the type without help from a torch.

The shelves were arranged in what would be called a maze if viewed from above, with naught but narrow passages between them so that upon entrance one could see scarcely two feet into the murk. The space was, in fact, so obscure that Herk, on one occasion, was startled on his way to retrieve a box of scarves when he very nearly collided with the buyer, his superior, who seemed to be pulling up or adjusting her panty hose. Her skirt was raised above her knees, one hand beneath it.

"Oh. Excuse me," Herk said quietly and hurried back out onto the sales floor, considerably flustered, not waiting for a response from the lady in question who returned to the sales area shortly, casting not even a glance at him.

This buyer was a woman of perhaps mid-thirties in age, of faultless grace, clothed always in the finest of apparel from the fashion department, dresses of gossamer fabric which seemed to caress her body as she moved. Her sable hair was long, pulled straight back from her face so that it created a polished helmet which ended in a long queue that swept her shoulder blades as she moved. Her face had the glow of youth and expensive make-up. She was attractive to be sure but slightly more ample than one who could be called striking. Still, Herk's brief glance, vague as it was, of her silken thighs had caused a momentary twitch in his groin. This caused him such dismay that he found it impossible to look directly at Ms. Randee—for that was her name—from that day forward.

It was near the date of Cousin Sylvia's birthday and Herkimer, in his constant effort to gain her approval, was anxious to present her a gift appropriate to her station.

She had come once to visit the ladies' accessories department with the stated intent to discover whether or not Herkimer, her charge, was pulling his weight. She marched into the department, her box-proud stride proclaiming due regency over her purview, and halted before one of the two younger salespeople.

"Yes," she said, a condescending curl to her lips, "I wonder if you might direct me to the supervisor of this department."

"The buyer just stepped away to a staff meeting," said the young woman.

"Oh, dear," said Cousin Sylvia. "Well, I was wondering, could you tell me something about the boy who does your stock room?"

The young woman was puzzled. "Why would you want to know about him?"

"He is my charge," Sylvia said, tilting her chin down so that she looked at the younger woman from beneath her eyebrows.

"Herkie?"

"Yes. Herkimer. And please don't call him Herkie." She did not want them too familiar with her charge.

The woman looked at Sylvia skeptically. "He's in the back I believe. I'll call him out if you'd like."

"Yes, do. But first, how is he doing?"

"Well, he gets here on time. He's quiet. He works hard. We quite like him."

"Good." At last Cousin Sylvia smiled.

When Herkimer appeared he found Sylvia inspecting some girdles of bronze and silver, ornate, carved images of flowers and birds, strung together of a length to fit loosely around a slender woman's waist.

"Oh, Herkimer," said Sylvia, "I just came by to see what accessories were sold in your department and wanted to say hello. Aren't these gorgeous sashes? I would love one of these to go with my favorite dinner dress. I would die for one."

Yes," said Herk. Though he thought them rather absurd he had learned not to contradict what his cousin and guardian proclaimed. He knew her reprisal would be a day or more of silent avoidance which had the effect of guilt on him.

"They are quite expensive aren't they?" she continued, studying the small tags secured to the belts which declared them worth two hundred and fifty dollars each.

"I can get a discount," said he.

"Oh, would you?" she importuned. "I would so like one. The bronze one especially."

Despite his few triumphs as a resident of the metropolis Herk had not felt that he had yet gained the trust—or was it the esteem—of his cousin's wife. And so, for the next twenty-four hours he fretted, conceiving a way, with his minimal salary of one hundred and fifty dollars a week, how he might come into possession of the artifact in question to be presented as a gift to Sylvia.

His discomfort was, in fact, greater in respect to her than to his supervisor, the buyer, whom he had observed with her pants down, so to speak. And so it was that he approached Ms. Randee to seek her assistance in obtaining the fabulous girdle.

"I was wondering, Ms. Randee, if you could tell me how much discount I could get on one of those metal belts. My guardian wants one very much and I thought ... well ... I thought ... I'd, well, get her one for her birthday."

She looked at him directly and he noticed for the first time that her eyes were quite abstruse; no feeling, no message came to him through them.

"You want a discount on a sash? Show it to me," she said and turned toward the rack which held the belts.

They walked a few steps and Herk reached in and picked off the bronze belt. It was a series of what looked to be leaves circled with stems of brambles.

"So you want to give her a belt of thorns." For the first time he saw what he took to be the hint of a smile to her corpulent lips. "You must dislike her."

"Oh, no. She's my guardian and she expressed an interest in these belts. She especially liked that one."

"Well, they're two hundred and fifty bucks apiece," said Ms. Randee. "How much do you make—I should know."

"A hundred and fifty a week."

"Then this thing will take almost two weeks of your pay."

"I don't care."

She cast a look about the department. The two other women were waiting on customers.

"And you want this one?" she asked, picking the brass belt he had indicated from the rack.

"Yes," he said.

"Come," said the buyer, belt in hand. "I can give you a special price." And she strode off toward the storage area.

Herkimer, while a bit baffled, followed her into the dim dungeon. She led him to the far corner, the most obscure part of the space, behind a row of crowded shelves where even the light of the ceiling bulbs did not reach. He almost ran into her supple torso for she stopped abruptly and turned toward him.

"Now," she said, panting as though she had run from a far reach or climbed a flight of stairs, "my boy, my shepherd boy, you shall have your desire if I may have mine."

He, too, was now breathing hard, so hard that he could not speak had he wished, for she had seized his shoulders and drawn him to her bulging bosom.

"Follow instructions and you shall have your sash. Raise my skirt and lower my panty hose."

Herkimer, because of her authority over him, complied. He felt the softness of her thighs as he ran his hands up to her buns and then to the elastic band at her waist. Slowly he slipped the lubricious fabric down her sleek legs all the way to her ankles while the appendage at his groin grew stiff and tight against his trousers.

"Now kiss me," she commanded, but when he arose and lifted his face towards hers she stopped him with a hand on his shoulder. "No. Down there." she demanded and pushed down on his shoulders. "My lower lips."

Herkimer was frightened now. He understood perfectly well that he was to perform cunnilingus, a thing he had heard about only in locker room talk, an exercise he had assured himself he could never perform, and here he was on his knees looking directly into his superior's privates. She gave him little time but took a spread stance, put her hands to the back of his head and pushed his face onto the hairy surface of her crotch.

Now, Herkimer had not been totally pure. There had been the country lass, his supervisor in a different way, so that he knew the location of the tiny bud which seemed to be the key to female ecstasy, and he thrust his tongue against it, nipped with his lips and drew a low, long moan from Ms. Randee. She pressed more firmly against the back of his head and, trapped thus, he continued to nip and lap until the lady's moan became more of a bray and he was fearful lest the whole of the department, indeed the floor, should be alerted to them. He did, however, confess to himself his own enjoyment, or should we say his instrument did so.

His fears were realized. Her cry of ecstasy was detected by at least one of the sales persons for a voice was heard from the entrance to their sanctum.

"Is something wrong back here?"

Ms. Randee quickly forgot her pleasure, placed a restraining hand on Herkimer's head and bowed her lips in a quiet "Sh-h."

"Hello!" called the voice as Ms. Randee shoved Herk away and leaned down to raise her hose.

"It's me," spoke the remarkably controlled supervisor. "We're looking for something back here and I ... I bumped my shin on the edge of a shelf."

Herkimer, also showing remarkable presence, seized the metal belt which she had let drop to the floor and secured it beneath one of the shelves as Ms Randee made her way to the exit.

He spent the rest of the afternoon sequestered in the storeroom except for two occasions, on one of which he was called out to deliver some accessories to the Bridal Department for Ms. Lillian, a pleasant, middle-aged woman, one of two regular sales persons who seemed to take an uncommon interest in Herk's demeanor. She leaned close to him as though to inspect his shirt collar and then turned away with an expression of disgust. It was not until several days later he discovered the cause of that look.

During the intervening days Ms. Randee made it clear to Herkimer that his payment was not yet complete. He was requested to minister her needs twice more. On one occasion she even zipped open his fly and grasped his appendage. She most surely would have instructed him to insert it had they not been interrupted again by a call from the floor for Ms. Randee.

Meanwhile, Herk had presented Cousin Sylvia with the bronze belt for which he paid the better part of a week's wage beyond his ministrations to the buyer. Cousin Sylvia was duly impressed, in fact, more laudatory toward, and inclusive of him in their daily plans, thenceforth.

"Oh, Herkimer," she exclaimed when he presented her with the belt, holding it toward her without wrapping or ceremony. She even grasped him and placed her lips against his temple in a fleeting buss but turned away to announce to her husband her good fortune before she could notice the flush which arose on the young man's neck.

It was, however, a full eight days before the repercussion to Herk's bargaining was discovered. It was on a Tuesday morning; all of the sales people who had been there on the day Herk and Ms. Randee had been called out of the den from their illicit liaison were there to observe, and the two of them were called once again, this time by name and to a specific location—the office of Mr. Sparse, manager of that floor.

They were directed by an elderly lady, gray from wispy top-knot to corded neck, with astringent demeanor, into a smallish office, handsome in its wooden trim but dark, with only one window which looked out upon the gray bricks of a neighboring edifice. There, behind a heavy wood table trimmed with carvings down the leg posts, sat a man of minimal stature, best described as skinny, with thick, fading eyebrows forming a wrinkled V above his spiny proboscis.

"Sit down Miss Randee," said Mr. Sparse in a voice which seemed to emanate from his nostrils. "You, too, young man." He cast his tight orbs in Herkimer's direction and the two sat in the chairs nearest each.

"Now, Miss Randee," said the floor manager with near delectation, "you are the buyer of women's accessories. You are retained not only to see that the department has the stylish and modish accouterments in stock but that it runs smoothly and without embarrassment."

"Yes, sir. And I believe I have fulfilled my charge," Ms. Randee stated, boldly.

"That means without scandal, Miss Randee," said Sparse.

"Scandal?" She affected a genuine surprise.

"It has been reported, Miss Randee, that you and this young ... young ... gigolo have been observed in licentious behavior."

"Licentious?!" Ms. Randee was shocked. "By whom?"

During this exchange Herkimer sat upright, showing no expression though he was, in fact, terrified.

"You were detected in the stock room performing sexual acts." Mr. Sparse spoke solemnly. "Do you deny it?"

"I suppose," said Ms. Randee, coolly, "that when I am instructing Herkimer in the proper arrangement of the merchandise Ms. Burroughs is conjuring some erotic scene for her own entertainment."

"She had, upon your exit from the stock room, smelled, quite distinctly on the young man, the effluence of female excitement."

"What the hell ...?" Ms. Randee's protest was interrupted when Sparse turned his scrutiny to Herkimer.

"Can you deny it?"

These words of interrogation brought Herk's terror to the surface. He flushed quite visibly. They were exposed!

"No, sir," he answered quickly and quietly.

Ms. Randee cast a glare toward Herk in a flare of outrage, but Herk kept his eyes focused on the supercilious expression of Mr. Sparse.

"Well," said Sparse, turning again to Ms. Randee, obviously satisfied, eyes arched in disdain. "What do you say to that, Miss Randee? A confession of guilt."

The change in Ms. Randee's aspect was immediate. Her face assumed a pallor; her lips were grim; she stared at Sparse. She said nothing but, after a moment, arose, turned and started from the room.

"Miss Randee," Sparse called at her, "you are dead in this store—and any other you might hope to connect with in this town."

As she stomped from the room Herkimer arose, supposing that he, too, was being dismissed, but Sparse called him back and with a more pleasant attitude asked him to resume his seat.

"Young man," the manager said when Herk was once again seated, "while I cannot condone your behavior I do not place the blame with you. She was your superior and I expect you obeyed her directives from a spirit of obedience. I can't imagine another reason for you to ... uh ... shall we say *service* that bitch." The manager had made a tent of his ten fingers and assumed a posture of guidance. "I have had problems with Randee from the moment I assumed my present position more than a year ago. Her attitude has been one of disrespect and insolence. She got away with it due to a special ... uh, relationship she had with the Chairman of the Board. This little piece of scandal should end that. So, my boy, you have inadvertently performed a service to me. You will find in your severance a small bonus."

With that Sparse smiled, leaned forward and proffered his hand. Herk perceived that he was dismissed, gripped the hand briefly and made exit.

His bonus was an extra week's pay which he applied toward refurbishing his wardrobe with the help of Cousin Sylvia who professed absolute knowledge of the proper attire for an undergraduate in a New England college. The scandal of his dismissal never reached beyond the floor of the department store, except, perhaps, for some gossip on other levels of that respected establishment, and Herk informed his patrons only that he had been dismissed, giving as reason a mean-spirited buyer who didn't like him. It was only three weeks shy of the date on which he was to matriculate at Occom College and so Herk spent the remainder of the summer stuffing his mind with the literature of the ages in preparation for his assault on the halls of higher learning.

VI

Occom College was to be a radical experience for Herkimer, a time of profound change, a completion of his persona. He had never before been independent, liberated from the immediate control of an older person. Of course, he had enjoyed considerable latitude when under the ward of the young woman in Clayton. That brief period had been a revelatory interlude which gave him a taste for freedom and he intended, now, to enjoy his release to the maximum. He made a conscious choice to exploit the fellowship available in his all-male dormitory and make use of other clannish organizations, though his early attempt at this proved somewhat intimidating. His natural reserve and modest stature also proved some hindrance though by Spring of his initial year this was completely cast aside when his immense skill with bat, ball and glove was displayed on the baseball diamond. He became a paragon of the freshman baseball team.

Occom had not long been a coeducational institution and, in the latter part of the eighth decade, the young women were still a minority and finding difficulty in assimilation into a school with such a long history as an all-male entity. Indeed, Occom had been in existence longer than The Republic and, being literally isolated in the hills of New Hampshire, had garnered a certain macho mystique which a great many of the male undergraduates attempted to maintain.

While Herkimer's relation with women had been considerable it had most often been on a guardian/ward basis. He had close affinity with few young ladies of his age and his only sensual contact had been initiated by women who, at the time, had held domination. There had been, of course, young ladies at Horney but he'd had little commerce with them due to his innate reserve. Strangely, this was to act in his favor with the male crowd in his dormitory.

His fair features, soft but not flaccid, accentuated by the bluest of eyes, with his powerful though slight physique, were quite attractive to many of the young ladies of Occom, especially after his prowess on the sporting field was broadcast. But his diffidence prevented him taking advantage of this popularity. In truth, he was in awe of women, frightened of them. His male colleagues read this as an indication that he held the fairer sex in disdain, that he was a bit of a misogynist, and applauded him for it. Herkimer, having no clue as to his acceptance by the men, did nothing to dispel this view until several semesters hence.

His first semester was un-momentous save for a few incidents of inebriate ribaldry he shared with some members of his dorm group. Camaraderie had not been one of his traits, either, but it seemed to be a strong tradition among Occom men, one not yet diluted by the moderating influence of the women on campus, and so he decided to immerse himself in it.

Women had been enrolled at Occom a scant four years when Herk entered. There were numerous of those carousing parlors, quaintly christened fraternities, but none of the sister societies. If the females desired raucous respite from the rigors of study they need be invited to one of the male clubs, for there was neither tavern nor lounge in the village where a student might safely seek pleasure. There was an inn but it was a rather courtly habitat enjoyed primarily by faculty, visiting parents and alumni.

Freshmen were not invited to join the drinking clubs until two months prior to the end of their second semester; they were, however, courted by the brotherhoods if they showed promise in athletics; there was some rivalry for distinction in securing the proper pledges. When early in the spring, before the ice had been dispelled and the sporting teams held their drill sessions in the spacious field house it was disseminated broadly that Herkimer was perhaps the pre-eminent freshman athlete; he became not just welcome but in demand at the frat clubs.

It was the custom at most of the societies that on Saturday night a keg of beer would be ordered up from the local supplier and a party ensued. On these occasions the fraters would engage in wild and often savage sport. It was not unusual that women would be present though not in great numbers for, being generally of a more moderate persuasion, few wished to engage in the raucous games, often raunchy and in bad taste. Herk was to learn why.

One evening in early April he and his roommate, Arnold Schwarz, were invited by an older student, Carl Madden, who lived down the hall in their dorm to accompany him to his club, the Alpha Kappa Psi, sometimes referred to as Awful Krapp and Pee. Arnold had proven to be a fortuitous chance in the roommate draw, an excellent mate to Herk. He was of agreeable temperament and his tutelage in Judaic tradition had created in him a strong moral fiber. He and Herkimer, though of diverse background, shared a common code of principle. So it was they found themselves, on the night in reference, alarmed at the episode which was to unfold before them.

It was a chilling night, dark by seven, the woods behind Occom were rank with haze while overhead a full moon gazed upon them through a halo in the mist.

"Spooky night," said Arnold with a shiver of his shoulders as the three crossed the broad, open flat of the College Green on their way to AKP.

"Yeah," said Madden, the frater, grinning with mischief. "A great night for some shenanigans."

The very word released a tremor of presentiment through Herk's frame. He smiled broadly at the promise.

By the time they arrived at the frat club the keg had been tapped and the merriment was well advanced. As they descended the stairs into the tap room they were hailed by the fraters with conviviality.

"Hey, Carl!" one of them called. "You brought a couple of neophytes. You're in for a big night," he continued, stepping close to the three, a tankard of beer in hand. "Get a beer." And leaning close in a confidential mode added, "We've got a couple of babes here tonight."

The room was well lighted. Along one wall was a serving counter at the open end of which, on the floor, was a beer keg with a pipe protruding from the center topped by a spigot. A stack of Styrofoam cups sat nearby on the counter and Herk perceived that they were to take one and fill it from the spigot. Carl did so and Arnold and Herk followed.

The basement room was rimmed by a low shelf lined with futons on which the revelers sat. As Herk served himself a beer his glance flicked to a corner where, on the futon, in recline, he saw a woman of such alluring beauty his eyes locked upon her anatomy, unable to move, though his sense told him this abrupt attraction was obvious to the other inhabitants of the close room.

He was a bit unsettled, too, by her obvious state of ease. She was clearly in her cups and appeared mindless to the license being taken of her. She was lodged between two large fraters; one had a hand above her knee, the other had placed one upon her swelling bosom. While Herk felt a twitch of excitation his moral conscience was quite more agitated by the scene. He moved to the far end of the room where another select of fraters seemed less vulgar. In their midst were two other young women, both of whom seemed much more in control of their actions and those of the men around them. Herkimer decided that one of these deserved his attention.

"Hello," he said, insinuating himself between two of the brothers to her side. "I'm Herk Hampton. Who are you?"

"My aren't you subtle?" she answered with arched brows.

This somewhat intimidated him and he began to draw away when she looked directly at him with a glimmer in her aspect and extending her hand added, "I'm Deeana Wallis."

"Hi, Deeana. Have you been here before?"

"No, this is my first time at your club."

"Oh, I'm not a member. I'm a freshman. I'm just a visitor."

"I'm a freshman, too," she said, showing her straight, gleaming teeth in a smile.

"Where do you live?"

"Over in Hotchkiss."

"I live in Morgan. We're almost neighbors."

For the next half hour he stayed close by the maiden's side, reveling in their ordinary chat and an occasional brush against her soft frame. He discovered she was, as he, of Mid-western origin—from Minneapolis, in fact, a city through which he had driven many times with his father on fishing trips to the northern lakes of Minnesota. While they were, as freshman, enrolled in only the required courses she intended to pursue a major in ancient history, a subject which held considerable interest for him.

"The Greeks," she said, "were so civilized—perhaps more so than we are today."

Herk was, may we say, enthralled. Of course she had been prepared in a fine, private school in Connecticut, a fact which also impressed our Herkimer.

While they were thus engaged the party had taken on a rather bawdy aspect. The young woman who had first attracted Herk's eye was now standing, quite unsteadily, in the far corner surrounded by males, her blouse unbuttoned, her bodice open, displaying a magnificent set of mammaries held tightly in a filmy bra. Two of the young men were on their knees before her entreating her like supplicants to more immodest exposure of her charms. They were pulling at her skirt, until she stood, woozy, clad in naught save her foundation cloth.

Herkimer was stunned. He looked away from this depravity. Neither could he look into the countenance of Deeana Wallis. He felt debased, ashamed even to admit, let alone display, his manhood. Then Deeana spoke.

"This is awful," she said. "I'm leaving here before she gets raped."

"I'll go with you," Herk said and, looking across the room, he saw Arnold gazing upon the lewd scene in disbelief.

"Come on, Arnold," he said, taking his roommate by the arm, "let's get out of here."

Without reply Schwarz turned and followed Herk and Deeana up the steps and out the front door. The cool night air was refreshing and helped assuage their anguish at the basement episode.

"I am shocked," said Deeana. "I would never have imagined that could happen here." And turning abruptly, as though to cast out the scene from her mind, extended her hand to Arnold saying, "I'm Deeana Wallis."

"Arnold Schwarz," said he, taking her hand.

"I'm happy to know you two are as appalled as I am," she continued, and, as they were just passing beneath a lamp along the street, the men could see that her expression was now more felicitous.

"Yes, it was appalling," replied Arnold.

Herk was still somewhat traumatized by what they had witnessed and kept silent as they walked toward the center of campus while the other two began a sprightly conversation during which Arnold learned that she was from Minneapolis, that she had prepped at Miss Privettes and that she was a member of the Wallis clan which owned and operated Minnesota Feed and Seed, a fact which impressed our country boy far more than it did Arnold who was from Long Island. Minnesota Feed and Seed not only supplied a great part of the Midwest with seed but made the nation's top-selling flour and numerous other culinary goods. Herk was in awe. Had he not been aware of her lineage he would undoubtedly have pursued her as a steady but was intimidated by her family position. A woman from a rich and powerful clan was above the level of a poor country boy, for the country was still in his marrow.

Nonetheless, Herk and Deeana became friends and whenever, in the ensuing weeks, she needed something only a male could supply she turned to him. He, on the other hand, neither asked for nor expected anything from her.

There was, however, one who did press suit upon her and that was no other than Herk's friend and roommate, Arnold Schwarz. Arnold, while a proper gentleman, was not so diffident as Herkimer. When he wished preference he spoke for it. He immediately asked Deeana to accompany him to the movies, she accepted, and from there forward they became a regular twosome, perhaps better to say threesome, for on most occasions Herk insinuated himself into their company and was able to do so because the lady seemed to approve. He always quit them before Arnold escorted her to her dorm, giving them every opportunity for intimacy if they had it in mind, and never did he press his friend for an accounting. Herk, did, however, despite his one ugly experience with the Alpha Kappa Psi, enter the rush for a spot in one of the Greek societies and found himself, upon completion of freshman year, a member, along with Arnold, of the brotherhood of Sigma Tau Rho, located on the opposite bounds of the campus from Awful Krapp and Pee.

Herk, as previously alluded, had been a paragon on the diamond and because of his celebrity in this his proficiency at studies had also become broadly known. He achieved a 3.8 grade average for the year, a feat seldom achieved by a first year student. Arnold, though his academics were rather less than average, had achieved some renown as a runner on the track squad and the roommates were a respected twosome. In fact, they were part of a familiar threesome for although Herk did consort with other women on the occasion of big weekends he scarcely had more than two dates with any one girl. No young woman of any self-esteem wished to be known as the unfamiliar fourth to the inseparable trio.

In fact Herk had never been so close to another as he was now to Arnold and, also, to Deeana. For the first time in his existence he had someone with whom he felt confident to share his feelings as well as conduct. The one thing he did not touch upon with Arnold, however, was his devotion to Deeana; for devotion was surely what he felt. In contrast Arnold never skimped in his disclosure of his most intimate relations with her. It was thus that Herk learned the venerated young woman was a virgin and intended to remain so until united in marriage with a kindred soul. This, of course, served to increase his devotion. It also made him the more reserved in expression of his esteem for her, even to Arnold. He could never admit to his previous licentious behavior with either of the vixens he had known—in the Biblical sense—and his recollections of those incidents caused him to feel unworthy, almost, of even the friendship of such a hallowed soul. In a word, Herkimer was smitten.

And yet he could speak with equanimity to Arnold about that fine fellow's bond with Deeana; he could accompany them on social events, sometimes with a date of his own. But from the time he learned of Deeana's chastity he never again tried to coax a female to coitus. In fact, after a few vexatious experiences with other women Herk's appetite for the female gender seemed totally assuaged. He became content in his role as the emasculate third in this congenial trio. In the beginning he even discussed with Deeana his relationship, or lack of such, with other women. She, on her hand, felt emboldened to pass judgment on these females, usually one of disapproval.

Deeana's resolve to virginity did not weaken Arnold's attraction either. As with Herk he was a young man of unusual—for this age—moral strength, so Deeana's chastity served to secure the tie.

"I am so lucky," Arnold said on one occasion when the roommates were sequestered in their sanctum. "Deeana is the nicest person I have ever known. She's smart and she's beautiful and she's not out after celebrity. I have you to thank for getting us together. You introduced us, remember? That night in the AKP house."

"I couldn't forget. Those guys must be the worst scoundrels on campus."

"Yeah, but if we hadn't gone there I wouldn't have met Deeana."

"I've always wondered how she ever happened to be in that damned place."

"Just like you and me. She went with another girl. She'd never been in a fraternity house before. How would she know what to expect?" Arnold gazed out the window, reflectively. "You know," he continued, "I thought you were the one she was interested in, but you never made a move so I did."

"I'm too much of a hick for her," Herk demurred. "She's really a classy lady. I'm just a simple country boy."

"Come off that, will you. You prepped in New York, in one of those classy city schools. I'm from Long Island, remember. If anyone's a hick it's me. I went to the town high school. Those people out there have about one tenth the sophistication as you city school guys."

"We're all friends, right?" Herk answered. "That's all that matters." Now, he too was gazing out the window. "I think that's the way it will always be with me. I'll have women friends and that's it. I don't think I'll ever marry."

Arnold laughed. "You can't say that. I've watched the girls go for you. One day you'll fall for one—just like that. Believe me, you will."

Herk had already met his ideal but could never confess it to anyone, especially Arnold. He could imagine Arnold and Deeana married with offspring and him visiting: Uncle Herk. Yes, Herkimer projected all this and they were in their second year at Occom, a year in which his reputation would go from that of skilled athlete, while nonetheless naive and somewhat a prig, to that of Occom's most gallant hero, one who led his faction from a position of trepidation and submission to that of strength and virtue in one valiant act of chivalry on which we shall dwell in the following episode.

VII

One balmy evening in the spring of their second year the three companions chanced to be strolling in the locale of the infamous Alpha Kappa Psi house when Deeana was suddenly possessed of a tremor which showed itself in a difficulty of speech.

"Oh, Guh...God," she stammered. "I cuh—cuh—can't guh ... go near this pluh ... place."

"What's the matter, Sweetheart?" asked Arnold, alarmed. "What place?"

"That place," said she, aiming her index at the brick edifice which housed the Awful Krap and Pee, and broke into a gallop, turning the corner onto Main Street.

When the two men caught up to her they found her sitting on a bench before the library breathing heavily, even gasping.

"What's wrong?" Herk asked. "You're reacting to the night of the near rape we saw, are you? That was a year ago."

Dusk had fallen and Deeana's eyes seemed almost headlamps so bright in fear were they.

"There is a monster who lives in that house," she said, still breathless.

"That whole house is a bunch of creeps," said Arnold.

"But there's one guy more evil than the others," she said. "He's the one who sets the standard for the whole house. They follow him—at least some of them do. He's got what amounts to a gang, about six guys, who do anything he says."

"What's his name?" asked Arnold.

"And what does he do that's so awful?" Herk added.

"His name is Anthony Barber," she choked out.

"The football player? That guy who's an all-league line backer?" said Arnold.

"Yes," she said. "And he has a gang which goes with him everywhere. Without them he wouldn't be so dangerous."

"What _do_ they do?" Herk asked again.

"They—he with their help—has raped more women than you can count!"

Herk turned to Arnold and saw in his friend's eyes a deep disgust, almost nausea.

"Why don't the women go to the dean or someone and warn the school about this guy?" Herk said after a moment. "Surely they'd do something about it. Kick him out, I'd think."

Deeana's tender visage looked to be at the edge of tears. She shook her head. "You guys can't imagine what it's like. If a woman accuses someone of rape more people—men, that is—blame her. 'She must have invited it.' That's what men always say, and this is still a male dominated school."

"Yeah, but the administration..." Arnold began, but she cut him short.

"You still don't understand, do you. When a woman is raped and the word gets around she's finished socially—damaged goods."

"But that's not fair!" Herk proclaimed.

"Dear Heart," said Deeana with a doleful smile, "who said life is fair?"

From that evening forth Herk bided his time awaiting the day when he would come face-to-face with this Tony The Barbarian. He became obsessed with the notion of a confrontation. So intent was he on satisfying his outrage that he was careless in the broadcast of his intention to "teach that scumbag a lesson" and these exact words were reported to Barber. Herk became the hunted man.

While Herkimer, Arnold and Deeana have been described as a threesome it is normal that their union should not be constant. And so it was that on one pleasant Saturday when Herk was returning to his dorm after an evening at the cinema, shared with other friends, he was accosted in the street leading to his quarters by three burly young men intent on diverting him from his purpose which was simply to retire for the night. They stepped from behind the corner of his dormitory building: one stood directly in his path, two posted themselves behind him.

"So you're the asshole who thinks he can teach us a lesson," said the guy before him, eight inches taller than Herkimer, his face, the shape of an inverted pear, displaying a contemptuous sneer.

"Why did you say us? Why not me?" replied our avenger.

"A smart-ass, too, hunh boys," said the man whom Herk had recognized as The Barbarian himself.

'Yeah," came a chorus of servility from behind, and Herk glanced across his own shoulder to see that there were now more of Barber's cohorts, perhaps five, gathered there. He could not take the time to count for Barber stepped close now, so close Herk breathed the musty odor of alcohol.

"I think he needs the lesson, don't you guys?" And without awaiting reply The Barbarian stepped back a stride and arched a blow at Herkimer's temple.

Had he been a bit keener Barber might have learned that Herkimer was a Karate Black Belt for it was generally known about campus, Herk having given a demonstration for one gym teacher. Instead, he found his blow deflected and bent double by a clout to the neck and a jolt to the groin.

Herkimer was not, however, to emerge victor. Instantly he was seized at both arms and drawn back, his abdomen pummeled, his face pelted, and as he lay on the concrete surface of the walkway the Big Man, having not totally recovered from his blows, stepped up to the stunned Herkimer and, leaning forward, hissed, "Now, fucker, be careful who you say you're gonna teach a lesson." And, giving our prostrate friend a boot in the crotch, The Barbarian moved away, into the dark, aided by his swearing sycophants.

Herk lay on the walk, retching from the kick in his balls, until two benevolent souls came to his aid. They raised him to his feet and paced with him, holding to his pits, until the malady in his midsection had abated and his full sensibility had returned. They asked to know the particulars of his distressing condition, to whom they might lay the blame, but Herk, already determined to bestow retribution, and having learned from this experience not to broadcast his intentions, chose to appease them with the affirmation that he wanted to make peace with his adversary and that it was best the incident be forgotten.

In order to make reprisal, however, he did recognize the need of assistance, and so, related the incident, in detail, to his comrades, Arnold and Deeana. They were appalled and as dedicated as Herkimer to a suitable revenge. Being in this disposition they devised an elaborate plan for justice.

"He's really nothing," said Herkimer, "without his support group. What we must do is get him away to some spot where I can catch him alone."

"Where we can catch him alone," Arnold amended.

"Okay," Herk agreed. "You can come and watch, but I intend to take my revenge, man-to-man. I can whip that S.O.B.'s ass. He's nothing without his troops."

Knowing Barber's intemperate lust they decided that, perhaps, they might lure him to some private spot by promise of carnal adventure.

"The Agora," said Deeana—the Agora being the open air theater named from Greek history, where, in days past, the awarding of degrees and honors were made. "If I can coax him to the Agora then you guys can grab him."

"You can't do it," Herk said. "Everyone knows the three of us are friends."

"I'll disguise myself," she said. "You know—dark glasses, tennis balls in my bra, a scarf around my head to hide my hair, platform shoes, a regular whore's get-up."

The discussion had begun to disturb Herk. He didn't wish to get Deeana involved in something dangerous and the thought of seeing her in voluptuary disguise was quite distasteful to him.

"Not a bad idea," said Arnold.

His roommate looked at him in disbelief.

"I don't think that's a good idea," said Herk. "That's too dangerous for Deeana. He might attack her before they get up to the agora."

"No," said Deeana. "I'll give him a note, tell him to meet me there—alone."

"Well ... maybe," said Herk, still worrying. Then, after a moment of thought, he added, "But what if he has his gang following him? He goes everywhere with that gang. They're his strength."

This posed another problem and the three were silent for some time, pondering.

Finally, Arnold spoke. "Well, we'll beat him at his own game. There are a lot of guys on this campus who hate that son-of-a-bitch. We'll form our own gang—ten, fifteen guys. We'll hide out along the path up to the Agora and if he brings his thugs we'll cut 'em off. He'll have to have 'em following a ways back. Deeana will make it clear he must be alone."

"Listen," said Deeana, "I'll make it seem that I'm so hot for him he will do most anything I ask. Just watch me. I'm not a member of the Occom Drama Society for nothing."

Deeana was indeed a talented Thespian. There was no need to doubt that she could pull off the charade, and, so, reluctantly, Herkimer agreed that this was a viable plan.

"There's still a problem," he said. "We have to kill this son-of-a-bitch. I don't mean literally, of course, but we've got to get him out of here. We've got to make him leave Occom."

"Or get him expelled," added Deeana.

"Yeah. If we can get him to confess all those rapes I'll bet the Dean will expel him," said Arnold.

"I've got it!" said Herk, perking up. "I'll take my little Walkman tape machine and get him to confess right there."

"Yeah! Yeah! Yeah!," the partners in conspiracy cried in unison, slapping their hands together in a conjunctive high five.

They planned the maneuver for the following weekend, a period when there would be no special event scheduled on campus. There was a baseball game on Saturday afternoon in which Herk was required to participate but that would be completed by late afternoon and the conspirators would have everything planned and prepared before that. Arnold found a bevy of men who expressed positive delight at the prospect of a campus delivered of the onus imposed upon it by the presence of The Barbarian.

Deeana tested the fitness of her disguise not only on Herkimer but on a few of her women friends. She showed herself to them, bulging at the bosom, hair wrapped tightly in a scarf, skirt of such short length it was an absolute scandal, with lustrous black stockings encasing her slender legs, all set off by ultra dark spectacles through which it would seem that she herself could not possibly have identified another. Everyone agreed that she was unrecognizable.

Her masquerade was so complete, in fact, that, before announcing it, she suddenly appeared in the get-up one evening, approaching Herkimer on Main Street before a restaurant to his complete consternation. So adept was she in the alteration of her locution that he imagined he was being propositioned by some strumpet come to ply her trade all the way from Boston.

And so, on the appointed day, thus attired, Deeana approached the large thug alongside the AKP house.

"I have heard," she spoke, slithering near to him and with most seductive inflection, "that you are the sexiest man on this campus. I have plied my trade from Washington to Boston and have not yet met a man superior to me in sexual stamina. I'd like to see if you could make me cry 'enough!'" She squeezed his arm. "Oh brother! Would I ever like to try it with you," she panted.

The monster gaped down at her, astounded. Then his face acquired a look of intrigue and a wry grin.

"You wouldn't be propositioning me, would you?"

"You could call it that," she said with a coyness that caused her to come perilously close to laughter.

"How much?"

"Oh, nothing for you. I'm testing—want to see if it's possible some guy can bring me to my knees."

"Well, I might just do that." He raised his eyebrows. "A little fellatio?"

She leaned in close, her warm breath on his neck. "Meet me at the Agora, ten o'clock tonight. I'll be waiting. And here are the rules." She handed him a folded note on which was inscribed, "Wear dungarees, a light shirt, no socks or underwear, and come alone. One trick a night."

Meantime, Arnold, as promised, had gathered a group of men, fifteen in all—he wanted to feel secure—who had united behind the declaration that they would finally free the campus of the Beast. At nine o'clock, led by Arnold, these stalwarts marched up the path toward the Agora, sheltered and cloaked by the dense forest which bounded the pathway and the craggy cliff which looked down upon the modest field which was to be the place of encounter. They were followed by Herkimer clad in his gym suit and shoes, his Walkman recorder clasped at his waistband, the small microphone taped beneath his T-shirt. He was accompanied by Deeana dressed as previously described.

The fearless fifteen, with Arnold, posted themselves out of sight and silent amongst the trees beside the road, while the other two marched resolutely to what was to be the scene of the encounter with The Barbarian. They had allowed one hour lead time in anticipation that Barber might have some suspicions and arrive early to investigate.

Deeana seated herself on the steps leading to the rostrum while Herkimer secluded himself to the side of these behind a large maple, close enough that he might reach her side with a few strides were there any unforeseen danger.

Sure enough, before many minutes had passed, down below, within sight of Arnold and his troops there appeared Barber. He appeared, at first, to be alone but within seconds a company of men followed. As they neared the entrance to the Agora, which came between two tall tamaracks, Barber halted and with a motion of his hand bade his followers hide themselves. He then proceeded into the grounds and his six thugs hid themselves in the forest.

Arnold had laid plans carefully. As soon as Barber had faded into the shadows of the Agora the fearless fifteen and Arnold crept upon the salacious six, seized each, three upon one, being certain to bind their mouths so that no warning might be given. The six were then forced back down the path to its beginning where Arnold felt secure his orders to them would not be heard and that they could give no warning.

"Listen, you bastards," he said in a low but articulate voice while their mouths remained gagged, "if you don't want to get in real trouble you just get the hell out of here and forget about this incident."

Immediately upon release the macho six dispersed like a flock of birds, scattering across the campus never to remark on the incident.

Up in the Agora The Barbarian approached the bait. Deeana, sitting serene below the rostrum, made no endeavor to rise until the monster stood directly over her. Then, as she stood, there came a sound of movement from the verge, three quick strides and the bully's throat was secured in the clutch of Herkimer, the redeemer.

Though Barber stood a full hand higher than Herk yet our intrepid champion, through the power in his torso and the stupefaction of his victim, was able to raise the devil from the earth and hold him some inches above the surface of the field, unable to move due to the anesthetic effect of the grip on the arteries of his gullet.

"Now you will confess to all your lowdown behavior," Herk hissed in his ear.

It is doubtful the scoundrel comprehended so near was he to being insensible, but Herk had foreseen this and, therefore, laid him on the turf, face down, drew his arms to the center of his spine and tied them together with a length of twine Deeana had carried for the purpose.

Barber, of course, began to shout for his support crew, but Herk silenced him with a swift, but not strong, kick to the groin.

"It will do you no good to shout for your band of thugs," Herk said. "They have been captured by our troops. The more noise you make the worse for you."

He then lifted the squirming Barbarian to his shoulder and proceeded to climb the rocky cliff which rose to one side of the Agora. Once on the precipice our liberator, after activating his recorder, raised the captive high over his head, face above the gaping pit and made his demand in a firm voice.

"Now, confess your sins against womanhood and purity."

"What? What?" The felon's reply was feeble.

"You know what I mean. Your crime against the women of this college."

"Rape? You mean rape?"

"Louder," the prosecutor demanded.

"Rape!" said Barber more clearly. "Yes, I have raped some women."

"How many?"

"A few."

Herkimer moved nearer the edge of the precipice giving his captive a clearer view of the rocks below.

"Many," came the immediate response. "I have raped many women."

With that our prosecutor rested his case. Herkimer lowered the Barbarian to earth, untied his hands, and, leaving him gasping there, climbed quickly down onto the floor of the Agora. Then, taking Deeana by the elbow, he proceeded, with her, from the theater.

Arnold's fearless fifteen took oath against revelation of the affairs of that triumphant evening and Barber's pusillanimous poltroons were humiliated to silence so the details were not widely known about the college. It was leaked somehow that Herk had counted coup on Barber and students awaited reprisal from the Barbarian and his troops.

Revenge was not to be, however. On Monday Herkimer sought, and was granted, audience with the Dean of the College and when admitted to the chambers played for his worthiness the tape of his summit conference.

"I thought you should hear this, sir," said Herkimer. "Anthony Barber's actions do not reflect well on the reputation of Occom College and I am proud to be a student here." Our liberator had practiced well his speech to the authority.

The Dean, as he listened, reddened and grimaced.

"And who is this man?" he asked of Herkimer.

"Anthony Barber. A junior I believe."

The Dean looked for a moment out the window onto the budding green of the foliage then turned his gaze directly upon our accuser.

"Mr. ... uh ..."

"Hampton, Sir."

"Would you consent to a face-to-face meeting with this Barber, here in my office?"

"Yes, Sir."

And so it was that, three days later, Herk found himself once more in the Dean's chambers along with Anthony Barber. He looked not at the scoundrel nor the scoundrel at him.

"Mr. Barber," the Dean began immediately they were seated. "I have serious charges against you."

"They're trumped up," said Barber. Obviously nervous and trying to cloak his fear he smiled.

"I would not be glib, Mr. Barber," said the Dean, normally a friendly sort but now severe. "I have here a taped recording of your confession to many rapes."

Barber shifted in his chair, still smiling nervously, and said, "But it was taken under duress."

"By this man?" questioned the Dean, looking to Herkimer.

"Him and his thugs," said Barber, almost snarling. "They ganged up on me. I don't know what they've got against me or what they hope to gain from it. Maybe it's just because the girls seem to like me."

Thus far Herk had not looked toward the accused but had maintained a serene study of the Dean's face. Now, however, he was surprised, for the Dean raised in his hand a folded sheaf of papers and proclaimed, "I have here written testimony from six women who attest to having been raped by you. I will not reveal their names as their witness was given under promise of complete anonymity. And, Mr. Barber," the Dean leaned forward across the desk toward the culprit, "I believe them. I have done some investigating myself into your behavior and I am appalled." He sat back in his chair, peaking his fingers before him. "Mr. Barber, you are expelled. You have until day after tomorrow to remove yourself from Occom College, and I will follow your progress minutely. If there is any further problem caused by you, you shall be prosecuted. Good day, Mr. Barber."

The Barbarian showed no emotion but arose and left the office and Herk arose to follow, but the Dean called him as he reached the doorway.

"Mr. Hampton, what prompted you to expose this man?"

"Sir, one of my best friends here is a woman, the girl friend of my roommate. She told me of Barber's offenses. She was petrified if ever we went past where he lived. I just thought it wasn't right."

"The young lady, I take it, is Miss Deeana Wallis?"

Herk was surprised. "How did you know?"

"She is the one who brought me these testimonies"—he held up the sheaf of papers—"which I ask you to watch me burn." And he took from his pocket a lighter, clicked it and applied the resulting flame to a corner of the sheaf of papers. He laid the burning bundle in a brass letter tray and the two of them watched it incinerate.

"Now you may report to your friend that you have seen the testimonies destroyed so that she, in turn, may assure her friends that their names will never be known except to themselves. I have already forgotten them."

Herkimer was satisfied when he left the office and the administration building but he was still apprehensive. Would The Barbarian try to take revenge? He could not do so without his company of rogues for Herk knew himself superior at hand-to-hand encounter and reasoned that they would now likely attempt to disassociate themselves from their dishonored and expelled leader.

His assumption was correct. He neither saw nor had communication from Anthony Barber and within forty-eight hours the man was gone from the campus. Herk, Arnold, Deeana and their friends took comfort in this.

VIII

After his triumph over the Barbarian the remainder of Herk's college residence was highly rewarding. He had, at the suggestion of Deeana, begun serious study of early Greek civilization. He majored in Philosophy and established a close attachment to the teachings of Plato, or perhaps we should be more accurate and say the teachings of Socrates as recorded by Plato.

His soul was to be permanently imprinted with the Athenian's admonishment, "Know thyself!" and that serious doubter's teachings that all we can ever know with certainty is ourselves. This along, with his father's previous counsel, "A man's word is his bond," were to effect his deportment during his adult life with few incidents of laxity.

Still, while he did become an all-league baseball player, was number two in his class for academics, close behind a brilliant woman scholar, and was awarded the Webster Trophy as the premier all-around student, he would be remembered by his classmates as the little guy who rid the campus of a monster.

He had been urged by his guardian, Cousin Joe, to stay on at the business school and study for a Master in Business Administration. He enrolled but after a semester, during which he saw that he would undoubtedly learn more about business by participation, he dropped out to seek employment.

He did come out of his semester of post graduate study with one tangible which would be of great value to him. Through diligence and one exceptional professor he became adept at financial book keeping. On completion of that semester he secured employment with a New York accountant and after six months of that he was able to pass the public accountant's examination and became a Certified Public Accountant. As the American society was then, early in the decade of the 1980's, entering the era of free market theology this was to benefit him.

He had little difficulty, with CPA on his resume and Cousin Joe's connections, in finding a situation with a large Wall Street concern. He began in the accounting department but within the year managed, through his pluck and intelligence, a transfer to the department engaged in Mergers and Acquisitions.

Herkimer had suspected that his friends, Arnold and Deeana, would announce their betrothal and embark in the world of reality a married couple. No such thing occurred. Arnold pursued his MBA also, not at Occom but at Columbia, and Deeana declared her resolute intent to follow a personal career far divorced from a life of urban commerce. At Occom she had shown herself to be remarkably proficient at mastering foreign language and, upon graduation, she signed on with an organization which gave their employees an intensive course in the use of whichever language that person chose and then sent them off to a country in which that language was the operative tongue there to instruct the nationals in English. Deeana, overcome by her romanticism and a desire to stretch life to its limits, chose to share her language skills with the natives of far off China, indeed, those in the interior province of Szechuan. She was to vanish from the purview of her two college mates.

Herkimer and Arnold remained in close communication. During the first year, while Herk lived with his relatives—no longer his guardians—in New York he made frequent contact with Arnold. Herk thought he was being compassionate when he tried to console Arnold at the loss of Deeana by assuring his friend that she would undoubtedly have a change of priorities upon her return from Asia. But the prospect of marriage had apparently never been high on Arnold's agenda. He seemed perfectly happy to be independent and sought his solace in the pursuit of other women.

After the first year, when Herk had taken his position with the Wall Street firm of Mortimer Brothers, the two former roommates met regularly in bars, restaurants and in Herkimer's newly engaged Upper West Side studio apartment, and Deeana's name was mentioned only in the course of reminiscence of their Occom experience and in wondering at her acceptance into the culture of China.

Perhaps it is time we had a closer look at Arnold Schwarz. At six feet and two inches he stood a full hand higher than his slight friend, Herkimer. While not of the powerfully packed physique of the latter he was, nonetheless, muscular and had handsome features, angular face, agate sharp eyes and lustrous black locks. He was, as ladies might say, a catch. While Herk was comely his attraction was of a more sensitive nature, and when the two were dining or imbibing together the ladies in the vicinity almost always cast surreptitious glances in the direction of Arnold.

In their second year out, of course, Herk was learning his trade while Arnold still pursued the theories of the market place in business school. It became habitual that, when the two friends met, Arnold would tell Herk of the hypothetical problems with which he wrestled and ask Herk's advise. In many instances, though not all by any means, Herk was able to give Arnold examples of a transaction in which he had witnessed the practical results and which helped Arnold to the correct solution of his assignment. In effect, Herk became Arnold's mentor and Arnold flattered him with praise.

"You know, Herk, you've always been smarter than I and what you did with business school just proves it. With your six or seven months of real experience you've learned twice as much about doing business than I have in two years of business school."

"I'm no smarter than you," said Herk, "but I do believe I made the right choice. Of course, if I'd never gone to business school at all I might not have decided to get my CPA. It would have taken me twice as long as it did."

"I think you're just smarter than I am," Arnold said, admiringly. "Maybe wiser is the right word."

"Baloney," said Herk and, growing embarrassed as he always did when complimented, decided to change the subject. "Have you met any women in that school of yours?"

"Yeah, quite a few," Arnold said, smiling.

"Then you don't miss Deeana?"

"Sure I do," Arnold said. "Don't you?"

"Yeah," said Herk. "But she was your girl friend not mine."

"Sometimes I wondered about that," Arnold said with a wry grin.

"Well, I've been wondering why you don't have a girl friend. All the girls look at you. Just like those two over there," Herk said, nodding his head in the direction of a table occupied by two women.

They were sitting in a coffee house but a few blocks from Herk's apartment—and from the Columbia campus—and the two women, who looked the right age to be students, sat directly at right angels to them so the men's faces were in clear view. As Arnold turned to look where Herk had indicated the women turned away and giggled.

"Come on," said Arnold, "let's get out of here," and he picked up the book he had previously placed on the table and raised a finger to signal the waiter.

Herk insisted on paying and after his pause at the cashier's counter he followed Arnold onto the street, grinning playfully.

"You don't like girls anymore?" he jested.

"Of course I like girls. But I want to do the choosing."

"Don't you know the woman always does the choosing?"

"That's not true. I do the choosing."

Herk shook his head. "Nope. It's the law of nature. The female chooses the male. Why do you think that male animals are always the ones with the elegant coats? To attract the females, that's why?" Herk was enjoying this. Arnold had no answer but looked, now, a bit reflective. "It's we humans," Herk continued, "who have turned the whole thing around, who have made it the custom that females must adorn themselves." He was on a roll, with insights, whether true or false he cared not. "And what do you think athletics are all about? The runner, the strong man, the thrower—all to show off our power and superiority to other males. And why? To attract the female." He paused to contemplate and Arnold, too, was reflective. "I think," Herk continued, "that women started all this dressing in finery, with baubles, showing off their bosoms, braiding their hair, only after the custom of private property became the rule among males."

Arnold was intrigued. "What do you mean? Why?"

"Because women wanted to be rich just like men did, but men, through their power, grabbed the property, made the rules. So women had to go after them, had to attract them. And then the fathers and mothers got into the act. They wanted to marry off their daughters to rich guys. They didn't want to have to worry about them all their lives. So the parents dolled them up in flashy clothes that showed off their figure, but only so much. Just enough to entice the horny bastards, to make them want to see more."

"Hey, I think you're on to something," Arnold said.

"No," Herk said. "I'm just stating the obvious. Besides that's pretty much over now with the liberation of women in the Twentieth Century. They can own their own property now. Someday in the future they'll probably own it all. They're so damned much smarter than we are."

"Oh, I don't know," said Arnold. "We've always had control of the property."

"Maybe not," Herk said, "Robert Graves says that way back before recorded history there were matriarchal societies, where the women ran everything. That's probably where the Greek stories of the Amazons came from."

Arnold laughed. "So someday we may live in a world where the women run everything, when feminism has taken over the whole damn thing."

"You don't have to worry, Arnold," Herk said. "You'll make out okay. It's the small guys like me who won't. I'll end up being some big woman's slave."

"Listen," said the jocular Arnold, "we all of us already are. Did you ever know a woman who didn't get her way? All she's got to do is flaunt her pussy at you. You remember that guy Alan Goldman who said, 'Women have all the power. They own one hundred percent of the pussy?'"

They broke down in laughter.

Perhaps it was fear of just such a predicament which kept Herk, for the first years of his career, celibate. He and Arnold never forgot this discourse and harked back to it on future occasions when they had been baffled by an encounter with a woman.

Herk was to have one beneficial encounter with a woman in his early years at Mortimer Brothers. While the investment game was still primarily a male sport women had begun to infiltrate by the 80's. One of the leader's in Mergers and Acquisitions was a woman, June Rosen, who was rumored to be the niece of Howard Schatner, a member of Mortimer's Board. While not on official assignment, Herk became, in effect, Ms Rosen's aid-de-camp.

June Rosen had early discerned Herk's ability to grasp the subtleties of any diversion in which they were engaged. Most people missed this part of him due to his stoic facade. He was, in business, as in other pursuits, unwilling to project his true acumen. And in that he was wise beyond his years, for his reticence served him well. When, upon listening in silence and waiting to absorb and consider the various possibilities in a situation, he finally sprung to the offensive others involved were invariably rendered inarticulate. He dumbfounded them with an intelligence they never imagined from him.

Ms. Rosen, some eight years senior to Herk, almost immediately, upon his transfer from accounting, became his mentor. She used him to gather information on companies. He became adept at reading and deciphering quarterly and annual reports. He developed a talent for predicting which firms might be ripe for a takeover or merger or which might be ready to assimilate a competitor, a valuable asset in the early years of Reaganomics.

She would then ask him to write proposals, one for the potential purchaser and another for the proposed acquisition. During his first two years at this process Ms. Rosen was successful in bringing to execution no fewer than eight sizable transactions. From these Mortimer Brothers realized a prodigious profit and Ms. Rosen a substantial bonus at the end of each year. Nor was Herkimer without reward. He received a bounty of fifty thousand dollars—a match of his salary—on two successive Decembers. He was convinced anew that he had been wise to forego the MBA. He had learned to read a balance sheet in business school, it is true, but in that year and a half he would have spent in the classroom he had learned not only how to interpret the annual reports but to apply the interpretations to the marketplace in order to turn a buck—several million bucks as it turned out.

He also learned much about the subtle art of manipulation—the shaping of another's intentions to one's own benefit—and he learned to do so while maintaining a convincing posture of innocence. For, indeed, he had never lost the ardor for fair play in which he had been inculcated by his father, the Judge and primal Presbyterian. He never promoted an idea with the purpose of besting the other fellow but only to benefit his associates.

By the end of his first two years with the firm he had secured himself a respectable position and his salary, with year-end bonus, had risen to a figure he had never ventured to predict on his entrance into the world of business.

By the end of *his* second year Arnold had completed his quest for the coveted MBA and taken a position, perhaps unwisely, with an association of petroleum producers with headquarters in Washington D.C. engaged, primarily, in the persuasion of law makers to the passage of legislation—or lack of it—which would auger to their benefit. He had enjoined himself to the Satanic pursuit of lobbying.

Herkimer was to feel, acutely, the absence of his prime source of sociality. While he was friendly with a number of employees at Mortimer Brothers most were either older and married or, if near him in age, involved with young women. He decided he had need of diversion, something to engage his mind, enable him to concentrate on something other than his lonely existence. He began to reminisce on the joys of his undergraduate days and to, once again, admit his attraction to Deeana Wallis. He recalled her affinity for language and resolved to become adept in a foreign tongue. In his business the emergence of Latin American countries was a topic of high interest at this time, and so he settled on Spanish and enrolled in a Berlitz course.

When he mentioned his evening pursuit to his supervisor, Ms. Rosen, she responded with delight.

"Oh, Herkimer, that's great!" she said, her cool, hazel eyes showing an unusual piquancy. "That's just what we need in this place, someone who can speak Spanish. I foresee a great future for us in the Latin American market. More and more U.S. companies are expanding into Mexico and South America."

Her reaction inspired in Herk a much more acute interest in this activity which he had originally begun only as a past time. Before three months had passed he was adequately proficient that he could engage the tutor in lively conversation.

"Meester Hahmpton," she said one evening after their appointed time was complete. "Wat you now must do ees go to a Lateen contry and leef for a time. Then you weel espeak Espanol perfecto."

This intrigued him. Here was a Latina telling him he might speak perfect Spanish. Being one who sought perfection he mused frequently on the idea. After a few months the idea of living abroad made his current circumstances seem tedious and he began to obsess about it. Leaving New York for the warmer climes seemed a fine idea. One day while languishing in his ennui he decided he must take action. He approached June Rosen.

"Ms. Rosen," he said with becoming deference. "I finished my Spanish course and now I can speak Spanish, not perfectly, of course, but well enough that my tutor told me if I went to live in a Latin country I would be able to speak it perfectly. Those were her words—if I lived in a Latin country I would learn to speak Espanol perfecto—perfect Spanish."

"That's nice, Herkimer. I would've expected that from you," her expression was genuine. She was pleased, her rouged lips curled in approval.

"I was wondering. Is there any way I could work for Mortimer Brothers in Latin America?"

"It's quite amazing that you should ask that," she replied. "I had been thinking that perhaps we could put you to work on Latin America." She raised her carefully plucked eyebrows. "Not <u>in</u> Latin America, but we might arrange it that you could go there for us from time to time—perhaps with me at first—to discover what opportunities we might unearth. There is a lot of interest in Latin America amongst our banking friends."

This did not totally satisfy our lately developed linguist but he reckoned it a beginning. Perhaps he could prove, on visitation to foreign capitals, accompanied by a senior member of the staff, Ms. Rosen, that it would be wise for Mortimer Brothers to establish themselves in one or more and that, with his grasp of the native tongue, he would be a logical choice to, at least, enter as a player in the enterprise.

And so it was that on one chill January morn he and his mentor embarked from Kennedy Airport on a flight to Mexico City, the nearest, and therefore most expedient capital in which to begin their inquiry. They, of course, had made appointments with some financiers and, through assistance of an acquaintance, June had at Amalgamated Fruit, with a tycoon in the agri-business of Mexico.

They arrived at Mexico City airport in late afternoon and were impressed by the agreeable warmth of the climate. Traveling through the city in a taxi on the way to the hotel, however, he was struck by contradictions. On the one hand the thoroughfare on which they drove was lined with billboards hailing the triumph of a consumer society, while, on the other hand, the neighborhoods seemed, if not squalid, surely at a high level of deterioration. Herk felt compelled to speak to his supervisor.

"Have you ever been here before?" he asked her.

"No," she said, raising her brows.

"What do you think?"

"Well, it certainly looks to be in the Third World." She shrugged. "But who knows what's behind those cracked cement walls—maybe nice houses."

"I don't think I'd want to live in one of them," he said with a shudder. He was not so sure that he would enjoy living here at all.

After a time, however, their driver turned off the main thoroughfare and they drove down a boulevard lined with houses, walled in to be sure, but in splendid repair as well as of handsome architecture.

"Now this is more like it," he said, smiling, imagining himself in one of these.

"Yes," said June. "Much nicer here."

"Como se llama este barrio?" Herk suddenly asked the driver.

"Este est Colonia Polanco," the driver tossed his answer past his shoulder.

"Gracias," said Herk.

June looked curious. "What was that all about?"

"I asked him the name of the neighborhood and he said it's called Colonia Polanco. Every city has a name for neighborhoods. I figured this would be no different."

The hotel where they stayed was a modern steel and concrete tower. It was the first time Herkimer had stayed in such a place. He had previously experienced only motels. His room was high above the surrounding neighborhood and he looked out onto the greenery of an expansive park. In the luminescence of the sun, low in the west now, and in the heart of the verdant grove that was the park, on a promontory, stood a stone building, like a fortress, a medieval castle surveying its domain. For several minutes after his arrival Herk stood in the broad window and gazed out over the scene. To the left, beyond the castle. were rows of more steel towers; to the right the greenery extended to what looked to be the brow of a hill, beyond the woods directly ahead he could see, at some distance, evidence of more large buildings, and beyond that, far to the South, a high ridge, a mountain range, not peaked but undulant against the clear sky. Herk was enthralled. He stood serene and silent until the telephone chimed.

The caller was, of course, Ms. Rosen who informed him of their dinner engagement with a Senor Fahtah. They were to meet him at eight P.M. and she suggested Herk join her early so they might prepare.

As they waited in the dining room of the hotel Herk was curious.

"The name Fahtah—it certainly doesn't sound Spanish. Is it an Indian name, you know, Aztec or something?"

"I asked that same question when my contact gave me the name," said his mentor, amused. "Seems he's from Morocco, Spanish Morocco. He's an Arab."

"Gee. I never thought there were Arabs in Mexico. It's such a Catholic country."

"My dear boy," said June, a condescending manner of address which irked Herkimer, a reminder of his status, "a person who is adept at finance is at home anyplace. Besides, Senor Fahtah's parents brought him here when he was quite young, they even changed his name to Carlos—a good Spanish name."

"What, exactly, are we to accomplish with him? I mean what are we asking of him, anyway?"

"Right now we're trying to get a feel for this market. They tell me he's one of the richest men in Mexico. He would probably welcome the infusion of some foreign capital. He's not of the old guard, not frightened of a couple of New York financial people like us. He wants to make money and doesn't care where it comes from."

"You mean we want to help him buy some companies?"

"Not necessarily. Maybe he'll sell us part of one of his. I understand he owns many companies here including a huge agricultural concern which not only grows plants from which tequila is made but then makes the tequila as well. Tequila is becoming a hot item in the U.S."

"Wow!" Herk was impressed. "This could really be interesting," he beamed.

They had some tequila while awaiting Senor Fahtah, Ms. Rosen referring to her watch as time passed and the Arab did not appear.

"I am told," Herkimer said, at length, "that Latins eat late. Perhaps that's why he hasn't arrived."

"I just hope the people who put me in touch with him knew what they were doing," said June. "I hope he doesn't stand us up."

"How will he know who we are?"

"I told the person I spoke with to tell Senor Fatah that I'd have a red bandanna in my hair."

"So that's why you've got that thing tied to the back of your head," Herk grinned. "I'd never seen you like that before but I wasn't going to mention it."

At fifteen minutes before nine two men arrived at their table, a taller one in coat and trousers which appeared to be a uniform, the other, a stocky gent with black mustache and shiny pate devoid of hair save a thin line just above his ears, and dressed in a business suit.

"Senorita Rosen?" asked the stubby fellow.

"Yes," answered June, extending her hand, bent from the wrist. "Senor Fahtah, I presume."

As he took her hand he cast a glance and said to the uniformed man, "Peude a vir," and the chauffeur—for it was clear he was that—made exit.

"This is my colleague, Herkimer Hampton," said June, nodding toward Herk.

"Buenas dias," said our newly self-appointed linguist and the short man grinned and corrected him, "Buenas <u>tardes</u>."

"Mr. Hampton speaks Spanish," said June.

"I see," said Senor Fahtah taking a seat with them.

"Well, I don't speak it as well as I'd like, obviously," said Herk, aware of his error.

"Meester—what ees eet—Hahm-tone?" Herk nodded and Fahtah continued, "That you espeak even esome ees unusual for a Norte Americano."

Herkimer smiled at the appellation, but Fahtah looked away from him toward June, his expression now austere as though to announce an end to amenities.

"Now, Mees ..." He was searching his memory for her name.

"Rosen," she supplied.

"Mees Rosen. You are here to investigate a possible investment."

"That's correct," June replied, pleasantly. "We have a client who might be interested in buying into one of your enterprises, particularly your agricultural business."

"Senorita, why vould you Norte Americancos be eenterested een agave plants," he looked at her with skepticism; "Unless, of course," he raised a finger, "you are thinking of tequila."

"You've got it," said the senorita. "Tequila is becoming a fashionable drink in the U.S. Quite fashionable."

"We have," he said with hauteur, "a distributor in your country."

"We know that," said June, undaunted by his imperious attitude. "We thought you might want an infusion of cash so you could promote your brand more effectively. You know, advertising, sales promotion. You could become a major brand."

Without pause, looking directly at June, Fahtah answered, "For feefty meelion dollars vee might deescuss."

Ms. Rosen looked for a moment at the center of the table, then up at Fahtah and repeated, as though in finality, "Fifty million."

Fahtah showed no change of emotion but continued to stare at June who, after a moment of silence, smiled. "And for that my client would own what percentage?"

Fahtah shrugged. "Perhaps ten percent."

During this exchange Herkimer looked on with a growing annoyance. He had, rather quickly, developed a distaste for Senor Fahtah. But June Rosen was not to be intimidated.

"Well," she said, relaxing in her chair, "let us order our dinner and discuss it."

"I have not time to dine," said the financier. "I must go on to a further reunion."

June, to Herk's delight, arose abruptly, offered her hand to Fahtah. "Perhaps we shall see you again." And he, seeing that he was being dismissed arose, took her hand weakly and, without a glance toward Herkimer, exited the site.

"That bastard," Herk said looking after the squat Arab. "Why the hell did he even come to meet us?"

"I think I know," said June. "He took great pleasure in insulting us—me in particular—because I'm a woman and women aren't supposed to engage in business. He is, after all, an Arab, undoubtedly a Muslim."

They ate their meal with little conversation. At one point June, gazing at the table top, said with dejection," I'm afraid this trip is a total bust."

"Don't say that," Herk replied. "We're not finished yet. I'll get that son-of-a-bitch some way or other."

This made June Rosen smile.

Next morning Herk had breakfast in his room and when June called to learn the reason for his absence from the breakfast buffet he was able to inform her that he had found and contacted a Mexico City branch of a New York bank and, after considerable travail, had managed to arrange a meeting with a vice president who was a gringo. They had an appointment for the following morning at eleven A.M.

"It's worth while to stay over an extra day I think," he said.

"I had planned two or three days anyway," said June.

And so the two of them spent the afternoon exploring the cultural marvels of the city, one of the oldest cultural centers in the Western Hemisphere. They began with the Zocalo, or city center, and its remains of the Aztec Temple Mayor, visited the floating gardens of Xochimilco and finished with the enthralling Museo de Antropologia, walking distance from the hotel.

Upon returning to their place of lodging they were exhausted and pursued no further recreation for the evening but retired after a brief repast. It had been, however, an edifying day for Herk. Not only was he enthralled by this encounter with the artifacts of ancient art, he also began to feel much at ease with his mentor, an ease he had not felt previously, for throughout the day she found it necessary to rely on him for communication with the locals.

The following morning found the two, having ascended into the summit of a steel tower which looked down on Paseo de la Reforms, ensconced in a spacious reception area, awaiting an audience with Mr. Robert Goulding of Metro Bank. They reclined on a glossy gray, leather couch while a sunny, insouciant receptionist smiled almost continuously as she responded to the relentless burbling of the telephone, sometimes in English, more often in Spanish. She spoke impeccable English, though with a pronounced accent, and Herkimer wondered that this woman, no more than a receptionist, had such education. He was to ask the question of Robert Goulding, the banker to whom they were eventually introduced, and received reply that English was a part of the required curriculum in the better secondary schools.

From this question Mr. Goulding perceived that Herkimer had a particularly inquisitive disposition and, there forward, directed the preponderance of his conversation toward our male friend. This, of course, prompted in Ms. Rosen a judgment that Goulding was no better than a misogynist and henceforth she maintained a silence which resounded in Herk's consciousness.

Nonetheless our slight friend persisted in his own investigation and they came away with a treasure of intelligence about not only the prevailing conventions in the Mexican market but also some specific data on Sr. Carlos Fahtah. Mr. Goulding seemed to take great satisfaction in discussion of the Arab.

"He is the front man for the current President and his family," said Goulding. "If this were in the U.S. media would be all over him and the President. But here high office is merely a license to—let us say—prosper. Which is not so say our Washington politicians are not corrupt. Here it is the way politics are practiced. The people know it and accept it. Which is not to say they approve. They get madder than hell at their presidents—after they are out of office. Some have even been what we might call banished to foreign countries for at least a period of time, usually until the president who follows them is also out of office. Then the people can vent their wrath on the latest ex-president and it may be safe for the earlier one to return."

Herkimer's eyes were agog. What he heard was unimaginable to him but he supposed he should believe it.

"And it's generally accepted by the people?" he asked.

Now, even June's interest was piqued.

"They say people get the government they deserve," she observed, flicking her eyebrows.

Mr. Goulding nodded to her with a pleasant smile.

"Mr. Fahtah, therefore, is not the man I would wish to deal with if I were you," said he. "He will take your money with promise of a share in one of his enterprises, but you will later find that the company in which you have supposedly invested will be a money loser. Your money will go directly into the pockets of Sr. Fahtah, the president and his clique, or, to be more precise, into a Swiss bank account. You would be wiser to find an honest Mexican to do business with.

"An how do we find one?" asked June.

"What type of business did you have in mind?"

She shrugged.

"Tell me," said Herk, "this Fahtah has told us that he has an American distributor for his tequila. Don't they have any interest in his shenanigans?"

"Hardly," said Goulding. "They simply buy the goods from him and re-sell it."

"But who is the distributor?" asked the persistent young financier.

"I couldn't tell you," said Goulding.

But a notion had taken root in Herkimer's mind. He had developed a loathing for Senor Fahtah and a determination to effect some revenge on the knave. As he and Ms. Rosen flew homeward he quietly engaged in deep lucubration, the object of which was the chastening of Carlos Fahtah and the delivering to his seatmate the object of her desire—Senor Fatah's expansive agave fields and the fruits of their potent nectar.

IX

Upon return to their office in New York Herkimer immediately did the small amount of research necessary to identify the importer of Don Diego Tequila. It was a company in Houston with the very American name of Wilson Imports. A small amount of further investigation revealed that Wilson was subsidiary to Distillers Combine Limited, the largest purveyor of spirits in the world, with headquarters in London.

Of course our young investigator was thorough, if not obsessive, as well as dauntless. He secured an appointment with the Director of Marketing at the New York office of DCL with promise of millions, if not billions, in increased revenue for any new owner of Don Diego and its agricultural holdings. It was, however, in all probability the name Mortimer Brothers which caused the DCL executive to assent to the interview.

Herk's meeting with the marketing gent was brief but not altogether fruitless. The man told Herk that their affiliation with Wilson had seemed profitable for both sides; that DCL owned but forty-nine percent of the Texas company and that Mr. Mark Wilson still owned the majority though he had ceased to exercise any direct management of the business and had placed the administration in the hands of one Manuel Rubiralta, a Mexican who had originally been hired to be responsible solely for the marketing of Don Diego Tequila and had proven so adept he was now President and General Manager of Wilson Imports.

Before the day was out Herkimer had made contact with Senor Rubiralta and, perhaps through an exhibition of his limited fluency in Spanish, obtained schedule of a meeting in Houston for the following Monday. Sunday he was on an airplane once again, not having shared his intentions with anyone, not even Ms. Rosen. He had, instead, requested a vacation day for that Monday. He did not wish the broadcast of folly should he be unsuccessful in his scheme.

The audience with Rubiralta was designated for ten A.M. and at nine-thirty Herkimer was sitting in the reception space attired ever so properly in a new blue pin-stripe suit with a plain maroon cravat, Windsor knotted, at his throat. Apparently, Senor Rubiralta had assumed gringo customs for it was precisely at ten A.M. that our friend was introduced to his office and person.

Manuel Rubiralta arose to take Herkimer's hand and Herk saw that the General Manager stood a whole head above his face. Rubiralta was tall by nearly any comparison, six feet four perhaps, with black sinuous hair and luminous, though almost ebony, eyes. He also was possessed of a sunny temperament conveyed through the amplitude of his smile.

"Mister Hampton?" Rubiralta's opening was in the form of a question.

"Si, Senor," answered Herkimer. "Mister Rubiralta, is it?" He had been very careful in his pronunciation.

"Correct! Correct!" beamed Rubiralta. "Have a seat."

He indicated the chair in which Herk was to sit and Herk noticed that he spoke English with scarcely an accent.

"Did I tell you why I wanted to talk to you?" Herk asked.

"Something about buying Don Diego, I think," Rubiralta answered.

"Yes," said Herkimer. "I don't really have a plan. We...uh...my boss and I, had a meeting with Senor Fahtah. A very short meeting. We didn't get much encouragement."

Rubiralta grinned and chuckled, "Carlos Fahtah is not what you would call a humble man. I suspect he was rather rude, wasn't he."

"He didn't want to talk about it, really. He said that maybe for fifty million cash we could buy ten percent."

"Which would get you nothing," said Rubiralta.

"But my boss ... well, she is pretty determined to start investing in Mexico..."

"Yes ..."

"I thought that you must know about business in Mexico in general and might help us."

"Why Don Diego?"

"We think that tequila will become a big commodity in the U.S. It already is, in fact, and we—that is she, my boss—got Fahtah's name from someone at a bank. Since we started there I wanted to pursue it at least until I'm sure it's a dead issue. Since I don't know anyone in Mexico I got your name from DCL."

"And did you tell them what you had in mind?"

"Well, not exactly. I did mention something about buying Don Diego. But I had just enough contact with Senor Fahtah to make me realize I should get someone closer to the business than whoever it was I talked to. Preferably a Mexican. So when I learned about Wilson and about you I thought I could start here."

"Hm-m." Mr. Rubiralta put one hand to his mouth and leaned over with his elbow on the desk. "Hm-m," he murmured again, obviously considering Herk's overture.

"You know," said Rubiralta after a moment. "I am not fond of Fahtah."

"Is anyone?" Herk smiled.

"The politicians," answered Rubiralta with a sense of resignation.

"That makes it tough, hunh?" Herk said with a shrug and made movement to arise, but Rubiralta stayed him with a motion of his hand.

"I did not say it is hopeless," said Rubiralta. "Let us think." He looked at the ceiling as though in meditation and continued slowly, "If we could get a politician directly—an important politician—say, the President ..." He looked directly at Herkimer now and grinned wickedly.

"Oh, Mr. Rubiralta ..."

"Manuel," the gentleman admonished.

"Yes, Manuel. And I am Herkimer, my friends call me Herk."

And thus began a friendship which was to—let us say, *wound*, Senor Fahtah—for he was too important to the financial health of the ruling party to be ruined or even halted.

Herkimer's sign had most certainly been in ascendance on that day for it happened that Manuel was close friend, University mate, to a man who had made the prudent and munificent choice of a career in politics and who had risen by now to a role as one of the President's chief advisers, the minister of finance, in fact. The plan was laid thus: Manuel would travel to Mexico City and engage his friend for what apparently would be a reunion of kindred spirits. During the course of a bibulous evening he would mention, incidentally, the possibility of a small fortune to be made in a financial adventure he had stumbled upon. He was certain that his friend's avarice would prompt a discussion of the deal which would result in an act of bribery and, if all went as Manual hoped, the purchase of the Don Diego properties, field and factory.

"This will need a considerable sum of money," said Manuel. "Considerable."

Herkimer did not blanch. "We'll get it. My boss is very good at raising money and I'm learning how to do it myself."

There were details to be straightened, most importantly the Mexican statute which mandated that any company headquartered in Mexico must have, in control, a Mexican citizen.

"That can be you," Herk said to Manuel; to which his new friend gave a look of resignation.

"I'm not sure I'm ready."

"Maybe you can find someone else," said Herkimer. "I trust your judgment."

"You have only just met me," said Manuel with a grin. "You are, perhaps, too trusting."

"I can tell," said Herk. "You could do it."

Before Manuel was dispatched for Mexico it was necessary that Herkimer discuss the details with Ms. Rosen. Rubiralta provided him an office with a telephone and Herk dialed Mortimer Brothers in New York and connected with June.

"Where the hell are you?" was her first inquiry and when he told her she wondered, "What the hell are you doing there?"

His explanation took several minutes for she, we will recall, had no previous hint of his elaborate scheme.

"Wait a minute," she said. "You are proposing that we go in there and bribe the Mexican government so they will talk Fahtah into selling."

"No, we don't go. I send my friend, Manuel."

"Your friend, Manuel?" She sounded disgusted. "Where did you find this guy? How do you know you can trust him?"

Exigency often brings cunning and Herk answered without hesitation, "Oh, he's a friend of my Cousin Joe. You know—Joe Wilson?"

"Oh ... yeah." Joe Wilson was a name of regard among the Wall Street minions. "And how much will it cost us?"

"For the pols? Oh, twenty, twenty-five mil." He had adapted well the casual attitude of Down Town.

"Well, let me shop around and see who might be willing to go it," she said, and her careless manner told him that she was now interested. "I'll call you tomorrow. Give me a phone number where I can reach you."

"Uh ... expense account?" He had suddenly remembered, he had done this, so far, on his own, without authorization. "Can I put this trip on my expense account?"

"You mean you haven't been? You ..."

He interrupted, "I was doing this for you. You wanted to have something in Mexico and we knew about Don Diego. I just thought ... well, I thought it better to pursue one we know about."

And so it was agreed that he should stay in Houston until they got something settled—or knew they could forget it. He gave her the number at Wilson and told her to ask for Mr. Rubiralta—a name she had difficulty understanding until he spelled it for her—and made his arrangements for an overnight sojourn. He told Manuel they would have their approval—or lack of it—in a day or two and made reservations at one of the better hotels—being now authorized to expend Mortimer money—and went out to investigate Houston, having first established that Manuel and he should rendezvous that evening for dinner and further discussion of their plan.

Herk's accommodations for the night were luxurious; their meal and conversation superior. Herk liked Manuel's geniality and Manuel Herk's innocence, his lack of guile. Manuel's previous experience with investment bankers had shown them to be somewhat artificial if not always deceitful. He was delighted to find one so sincere and candid. From the start Herk had come straight to the point and Manuel presumed that this was probably his youth and brief experience in the regimen. By the end of the evening they had agreed that, should their efforts be successful and DCL should, in the end, own Don Diego, Manuel would move back to Mexico City, or better perhaps, to Guadalajara, in the agricultural state of Jalisco where mile upon mile of agave plantations lay, and from there administer the operation of the enterprise. Herk, on the other hand, had agreed that, should it be necessary, during the ensuing weeks, for Manuel to be absent from his duties here at Wilson for any length of time, that Herk would come back to Houston and assume Manuel's daily duties as manager.

"But how can I do that?" Herk had wondered. "I don't know anything about your business."

"Nothing to it," said Manuel. "We'll start tomorrow. I'll tell you what's happening. You see, while I'm gone—even if it takes two weeks, and it won't— you would merely have to say yes or no, give go or no-go decisions. I'll tell you about everything that's pending and what my response to each would be. I'll make sure everyone knows you have my authority. If anything really baffles you just call me in Mexico."

"You don't have someone working for you who could do that?" Herk asked.

"We have a very minimal staff. They're all salesmen except for me and my assistant, Miss Blue."

And so it was that Herkimer reluctantly agreed.

Next day noon came and passed without word from Ms. Rosen and Herk was becoming uneasy. When, at a few minutes before one, the call came and Herk was summoned to Manuel's office to take it he was jittery. The calm voice of June Rosen restored some serenity.

"What time is it there, anyway?" was her first observation.

"About one o'clock," Herk answered.

"Oh! I'm sorry. It's your lunch time."

"That's okay. I couldn't eat until I heard from you."

"Well, I've got good news and bad news. First, the good news; DCL would love to own controlling interest in Don Diego. The bad news is that they don't think that's possible with that bastard Fahtah. He's a dangerous man. He'll just screw them out of their money and keep control. That's what my contact at DCL said."

"We don't intend to have him around," said Herk. "We'll kill the son-of-a-bitch."

"You think you can?"

"I know we can," said Herk with determination. "Can you get the money?"

"Oh yeah, I have a bank that will invest in almost anything in Mexico and they know DCL's track record. None better."

So it was decided. Herk went back to New York that afternoon. He upgraded to first class with Ms. Rosen's authorization. As it transpired he found himself on a flight which had originated in Mexico City and seated next to a young Mexican gentleman of thirty something, a businessman, who proved talkative, in fact, garrulous.

He began by observing that he had not seen Herkimer on the flight from Mexico City, to which Herk admitted but remarked that he had been there no later than the past week. Upon inquiry the young man extracted from Herk something of the purpose of his meeting and, upon learning that Herk had actually met with Senor Fahtah, was in awe. Fahtah, he offered, was one of the most powerful financiers in Mexico, feared by all. Herk became the more resolute in his determination. Now he had a confirmed dragon to kill—or for Manuel to kill.

In the following week Herk was very impatient, agitated. He called Manuel Rubiralta each morning and afternoon. In the early days of the week his friend was pleasant but not very satisfying. He was having difficulty getting through to the Finance Minister. As the week progressed Manuel became jocular, teasing Herk for his lack of trust.

Meantime Cousin Joe, with whom Herk had not communicated in several weeks, called to suggest that the two should lunch together and so they met at a new restaurant located in TriBeca which Joe suggested.

"I've been wondering a lot about you," Joe grinned across the table. "How are you doing in that place? What are you doing these days?"

Herk declared, without enthusiasm, that he thought he was doing adequately.

"What's wrong? Don't you like it?"

"I'm not sure I should be in this business."

"Why not?" Joe was disturbed. "It's the best way I know to make money. As the financier and, later, statesman, Bernard Baruch, said, 'If you want to make money you should be in the business of making money.' That's just where you are."

"I'm not sure that's all I want to do. I want to make enough to live on, but there are things about this business I don't feel comfortable doing."

"Like what?"

"Like bribery."

"Bribery?" Joe frowned. "You mean paying some guy to help you get something done? That's not bribery. It's just the way you pay a contractor to build you a house."

"But when it's a government official?" It became clear that Herk had been engaged in serious reflection on the negotiations he had put in motion and the ethics involved.

Joe's eyebrows raised in surprise. "You're involved in Washington?"

"No," said Herk. "In Mexico."

"Mexico!" Joe began to laugh. "What could you be doing with the Mexican government?"

And so Herkimer confessed to Cousin Joe the machinations he had set in motion south of the border; he told him about his new friend Manuel, whom he praised highly, and about Manuel's friend the Minister of Finance to the Mexican President.

Joe listened, fascinated, and when Herk had finished he effervesced. "Here you are just two years into the business and already you're involved in foreign intrigue." He laughed again.

"You think it's funny?" Herk was disconcerted.

"Not really funny," Joe said. "I'm just amazed and pleased at how fast you're picking up the ways of economics."

This did not assuage our Herkimer. He continued to fret on the propriety of his actions.

"Don't worry a bit," said Joe. "I have a friend, Dan Doolittle, who was Ambassador to Mexico. He's told me tales of the Mexican government, the President and the ruling party, which make your small scheme an act of moral virtuosity. Don't worry another second. Go ahead and make your company some money. They'll reward you."

But Herk could not escape the feeling that he was doing wrong. Still he felt an obligation to pursue to conclusion his dealings with Senor Fahtah and Don Diego S.A de C.V. He felt somehow morally obligated to his employers. They were paying him to help expand their profit, and it had been he, after all, who had involved Manuel Rubiralta and, together with him, had arrived at the plot to enlist the help of a government official. As he weighed the cost of culpability on his conscience he decided either action—backing out or continuing—would exact about the same quantity of guilt. He didn't want to desert his new friend Rubiralta and he would get satisfaction from being able to deliver to June Rosen what she so highly coveted. She had been kind to him, nurturing him in the lofty spheres of finance. He decided to persevere.

On that Friday Manuel called to inform him that he was to meet with his friend at Finance on the following Tuesday and asked if Herk would return to Houston to take up his brief residency as manager pro-tem of Wilson Distributors. He embarked on Sunday and was met at the airport by Rubiralta who seemed in high spirits.

Next morning Manuel introduced Herk to the few employees and told them that Herk was from DCL in New York and would be in charge the few days he, Manuel, would be absent. He neither told them his destination nor gave date of return. He did, however, give Herk a telephone number where he could be reached in Mexico. This proved fortunate for Herkimer phoned Manuel no fewer than three times the first day to receive instructions on decisions he was called upon to make. On the third day Rubiralta phoned Herkimer with a rather disturbing report; his friend, the Finance Minister, was loathe to consider Manuel's proposition. Fahtah, it seems, held more power with the President as a consequence of his financial "advise" than even the Finance Minister. The

Finance Minister was afraid to advance any proposal opposed to that of the cunning Arab. Manuel was stymied.

Herkimer was disturbed. He had continued the pursuit with misgivings; he now wondered if his conscience had not been influenced by a higher power, a moral force outside his rational cognition.

He closed the door to the office in which he was ensconced and meditated. He was alone, undisturbed, for perhaps an hour until a revelation came to him. He had already gone too far in these machinations to avoid culpability and his good reputation at Mortimer was at risk. He must try one more time to effect the coup. He remembered that Cousin Joe had alluded to a friendship with a former ambassador to Mexico. He immediately, without further debate, phoned his cousin.

Joe did not seem surprised. "I had hoped you might call me," he said. "I have already been in touch with my friend Dan Doolittle. He had a chuckle over your scheme."

"Well, what should I do now?" asked Herk.

He could hear the humor in his cousin's voice as Joe replied, "Don't worry about it. I think Dan can help. When he was in Mexico he was friendly with the current president."

Herk immediately phoned Manuel but Manuel was not at the number Herk had called before.

"Donde el este?" Herk was grateful for his limited Spanish. The woman on the line gave him a number where she thought he might be reached, but when he phoned that number he was, once again, informed of Manuel's absence. It was now just two P.M., an hour at which, he recalled, people in Mexico City paused for *la comida*, their mid-day repast. He became agitated, flushed with anxiety. Suppose Manuel had capitulated, become resigned to the belief that their plan had failed; suppose he had already departed Mexico. Fretting thus Herkimer decided that, perhaps, some nourishment might restore a modicum of composure. He repaired to a restaurant in the vicinity and there made a decision, almost never taken, to imbibe in the very potion for which he suffered his current anguish. He ordered a marguerita cocktail to be made with Don Diego Tequila, hoping perhaps, that these spirits might invoke others to intercede on his behalf with the Grand Master of Fortune. He could do no more than place himself in the hands of God and the curative puissance of alcohol, which, if it could not effect this, would, at the least, alleviate his angst.

As he took his first sip of the marvelous emerald liquid he found it quite unlike other cocktails he had tasted. They had repelled him; this inspired a desire for more. When he returned to the office at four P.M. he did so unsteadily. Before closing himself into the room he was advised by the assistant that no calls had come for him. He awoke some hours later to a darkened chamber, resting on a couch. The door was still closed, the lights in the building opposite were gleaming in the murk. He arose, a twinge of pain behind his eyes, switched on a light and gazed down at the telephone, silent and serene. You culprit! Why don't you ring?

He looked at his watch. It was eight fifteen P.M. That phone would sound no more during this evening. Herkimer felt despair. Tomorrow Manuel would return to announce their failure. Herk's first shot at the big one had been a miss. He left the office building and walked the seven blocks to the hotel transporting the only fruit of his great scheme, the residue of Don Diego which seemed to be lodged in his skull causing a delicate nausea. He took no further nutriment but collapsed on the bed to a night of irregular repose, tormented by retributive dreams.

The following morning he was sluggish in his efforts to reach the office, certain that, upon arrival, he would discover Manuel ensconced in his customary quarters. When he was disappointed in this he could do no more than to sit and await the bad news.

At eleven A.M. the chiming of the telephone roused him from a reverie into which he had fallen and he seized the receiver. It was Manuel and his "bueno" was surprisingly cheerful.

"Did you call someone down here?" Manuel asked.

"No." Herk was puzzled.

"Well, something happened," bubbled Rubiralta. "The Minister has changed his mind. We are in the process of arranging the details of the purchase."

"What happened to Fahtah?"

"I believe he was told to withdraw quietly with the ten or fifteen million they promised him."

"Ten or fifteen million dollars?" The magnitude startled Herkimer. "I'd think that would satisfy anyone."

"A pittance to Senor Carlos Fahtah," Manuel answered. "But they have apparently told him to take it and shut up." He turned curious. "But I can't imagine what suddenly changed everything. My friend, the Minister, called me last night and told me that he had spoken to a trusted gringo friend who told him it sounded like a good deal and they ought to take the offer."

Of course! Herkimer was now certain that Cousin Joe had induced his friend Dan Doolittle to intervene. The transaction was assured.

Manuel told him it would require a day or two more to negotiate the particulars, that he expected to be home in Houston by Friday, and prevailed on Herk to be in the office so that he might deliver the precise details to his boss at Mortimer.

The details, that part of them to which the gringos were exposed, came to this: for fifty million dollars DCL might acquire controlling interest in Don Diego.

"They stipulated, however, that Fahtah, as a Mexican citizen, continue to manage the business," said Manuel.

"Impossible!" cried Herkimer, but Manuel raised his palm to pacify his friend.

"I talked them out of that," Rubiralta continued. "I told them that was not possible; the gringos would not hear of it, and, so, they agreed that I should return to Mexico and assume the title of Managing Director."

Herk looked earnestly into Rubiralta's eyes and after a moment, perceiving no skepticism, asked, "And do you really trust them? You don't think that, once the deal is made, they'll try to bring Fahtah back to manage you?"

"They can't. DCL owns the business now. And I told them I could not work with Fahtah, that he could have nothing more to do with Don Diego. I used my Jewish heritage and his Muslim faith as the reason." Rubiralta's smile broadened. "And you see I have a bit of hidden confidence on the Finance Minister. I am aware of his family's descent from Abraham."

Herkimer was perplexed. He knew nothing of this Abraham and Manuel had delivered this passage as though Herk were privy to a secret. When Rubrialta perceived Herk's consternation he began to laugh.

"You don't get it?" he questioned, chuckling still. "Abraham. The patriarch all Jews call father."

And Herk got it. "So he's Jewish?"

"He and I. The difference is that his family came over here many generations before mine. Mine came from Russia in the Twenties. Rubinskaya we were and became Rubiralta to sound more Mexican. The Finance Minister is Fernandez, couldn't be more Spanish, right? And he is. You see he is a Sephardic Jew whose family came here more than four hundred years ago to escape the Spanish Inquisition. Thousands professed Catholicism but kept their traditions in secret and do so right down to this day."

"I still don't understand. Why does that matter?"

"Ah-h, you see, the Mexicans are much better at hiding their prejudices than you gringos. While the Church was supposedly thrown out of government by the Revolution, still the politicians are all Catholic and the President's circle more than most."

"I guess I understand—kind of," Herk said, though still perplexed. Then he added, "But you've done fine, apparently. You worked in Mexico before coming to the States, didn't you?"

"I actually worked for Fahtah. That's how I know I can't do it again. It is complex, no?" Herk noticed the Spanish idiom stealing into Manuel's speech.

"It is fine, amigo, for Jews to progress in commerce. That is, after all, what we are good at, correct? We help to advance the politicians' economy, but to actually participate in government, oh no. That is for the pure of heart Catholic. Investigate, my friend. See if you find, in the ruling party, a Protestant. Few if any."

Herkimer was being granted a glimpse into the craft of Mexican politics.

"The *ruling* party?" Another conundrum for him to ponder.

"The PRI. The ruling party."

"The *ruling* party? But it is a democracy. In a democracy the people rule."

"So they would like it to appear," Rubiralta smiled. "My friend, since 1928 there has been but one party in control of all Mexico. The others exist only for appearance. The President appoints his successor. The PRI, the Institutional Revolutionary Party, rules all."

Herkimer nodded, pondering what his friend had revealed.

"And I have thought," he said at length, "that our two parties had all together too much control in the States." Then, after further deliberation, he added, "So you have broken through to those in control."

"In complete control," said Rubiralta, and, after a moment's silence, he added, "It is all done with the mordida, the bite, or bribe as you would call it. None of the fifty million, mi amigo, will go into the business but rather into the pockets of the politicians. Our president will be more wealthy by perhaps twenty million dollars. My friend, Fernandez, also will be considerably more rich."

"And you?" Herk could not refrain from asking.

"Very little," said Rubiralta with a shrug. "A finder's fee is all—and, of course, a lucrative job." He grinned broadly. It was not until some time later in his career that Herkimer acquired any propensity for distrust within his guileless nature, but some months later he wondered at the magnitude of Manuel's "finder's fee" and whether it was not, more accurately, a seal on his lips.

When he returned to New York the negotiations were completed. June secured the money from one of the large mercantile banks, and she and Herk accomplished the purchase of Don Diego for DCL. During these negotiations Herk learned that in Mergers and Acquisitions nothing is concluded until the final signatures are subscribed to the document of acquisition. Due to the pertinacity of the DCL Chairman Herk was once more dispatched to Mexico. This time he was sent to Guadalajara, the capital of the State of Jalisco, where the agave plantations and the distillery of Don Diego were located. He was to inspect the production facilities and procure a government record of the deed to the land, on which was specified the exact co-ordinates of the properties. If necessary he was to find a surveyor and verify the exact magnitude of the purchase.

He found the city of Guadalajara to have more the aspect of urban California than Mexico City. The distillery was in a town several miles distant from Guadalajara, a small town named, appropriately, Tequila; thus he learned the origin of the name for one of Mexico's most famous exports. There he introduced himself to *el gerente* of the distillery who had been advised by Rubiralta of his impending arrival. He was escorted through the plant. He found the sight of large cauldrons in which the juice of interest was cooked, but he was especially impressed with the huge store house filled with a plethora of giant barrels in which the fermentis delecti was being aged. El Gerente also took him on a tour through the agave fields, acre after acre—or as he learned—hectare after hectare. The agave was a strange looking plant which, when viewed in the field, as a panorama, gave the impression of thousands of up-ended spiders with protruding legs.

Herk's procurement of the deed was neither so speedy nor so facile. He was compelled to seek out an abogado—which he discovered was the title given a lawyer. Let it suffice that after several days of waiting, and the proffering of no small number of mordidas, he returned to New York transporting a sheaf of papers purported to be a copy of the deed to the land and which was, after examination by the DCL legal staff, accepted as valid. Herk's first venture into the field of international finance came to a successful conclusion.

Ms. June Rosen was elated and professed immense gratitude to Herkimer for his "assistance" in the matter. She made promise of promotion and success for her tireless trooper. The rumor reached his ear, some weeks later, that Mortimer Brothers had received a commission of some three million dollars from which a handsome bonus was paid to Ms Rosen. Perhaps, Herk ruminated—not without irony—that he might receive his *mordida* at year-end.

X

The tequila ordeal had been a physical and strategic trial for Herk, but more devastating was the moral implication. The political machinations had disturbed him and he was to contemplate, at considerable length, the advisability of continuing in this field. He lived in silent torment for several weeks until, subdued by his anguish, he confessed his doubts to his superior, Ms. Rosen.

"How long have you been with us?" she asked, giving the impression of concern.

"Almost two years," he said.

She smiled and nodded as though in possession of some arcane knowledge.

"Yes," she said. "Very often this happens in the early stages of a career. People have doubts about their ability to keep up with the great demands. It happened to me. I know what you're going through. Give it a couple of more years. Your doubts will go. You'll see." He was sitting beside her desk, the corner protruding between them, and she leaned forward and put her hand on one of his which was gripping the arm rest, a gesture of intimacy she had never before displayed. "You've got just the brains and gumption that makes it big in this business."

Herk saw this as a fine gesture of amity, though perhaps it was not so much that as a desperate desire on the part of June Rosen to retain her reliable squire. Herk stayed.

Perhaps to show that she was not totally vulpine in typical Wall Street fashion his next semi-monthly stipend included a sizable boost, a fact Ms. Rosen did not let pass un-remarked. She made presentation of the augmented draft in another personal interview.

"I told you that you have a great future here," she said, "and the management agrees. And," she hastened to add, with a bit more emphasis, "in another year or so you'll be making twice this and be glad you stayed on."

Herkimer thanked her adequately and retreated from the office smiling. But in the following months and years, in moments of meditation, he would ask himself, "Is this why we exist, why we toil; for money, that alone?" This he would continue to ask himself for several years to come.

His next two years were productive if not spiritually gratifying. Twice more he traveled to Latin America, once to Mexico and once to Argentina where he effected the purchase of that nation's largest soft drink bottling company for an ex-patriot American living in Buenos Aires. This transaction was quite beneficent to Herk, personally, as the American helped him to invest in the acquisition. His portion of twenty thousand dollars could scarcely be noticed in the calculations, yet by the end of the first year his investment had multiplied in value ten fold and Herkimer, being the cautious son of cautious mid-western stock had realized his profits and, via bank draft, transferred more than two hundred thousand dollars into a Swiss bank account. This sale proved expedient. The ex-pat was forced into insolvency by the distribution company which simply collected money from the retailers and failed to pass it on to the bottler. He was forced to sell his company to the lowest bidder.

Herkimer emerged from this debacle, however, more esteemed than before. He had investigated every aspect of the deal and had, indeed, warned the ex-pat American of the deceitfulness of the distributor. He had also expressed his doubts to the U.S. bank which had advanced the loan to the ex-pat and they, in turn, had transferred the debt to a bank in the Bahamas which, finally, was forced to write if off as a sizable loss.

It was during this time that Mortimer Brothers decided that, instead of taking haphazard risks, they should create a Latin American Division and while Herk was too green to be director of this group he was appointed sub-director. He was to research possibilities and contract deals. By now he was remunerated at a rate he had scarcely imagined in his early apprenticeship; his year-end bonus now matched his annual wages.

His director was a man who, if not yet forty, was nearing that seminal age, a thin man named Frank O'Dwyer who, without doubt, had developed his emaciated demean from indulgence of his edacious appetite for alcohol. While he did not often appear drunk yet he always carried with him the whiff of spritis fermenti and upon occasion he would waft off into soliloquies employing the vernacular of his ancestral tongue.

"Sure and ye'd better be on y'r toes fer this'n, me boy, fer t'is certain it'll put more'n a nickel in the purse a them that grants y'r wages." Herkimer was generous in his regard for his boss, however, for, while he did not approve the over-indulgence in spirits, he saw in the man a compassion shared by few in the palaces of high commerce. O'Dwyer was a humane individual who seemed, genuinely, to care for his staff. Herk regularly let pass without remark those occasions upon which an associate would refer to their manager as "The Drunk," for it was a subject of conjecture why the powers of Mortimer would tolerate, as manager of a department, a man of such intemperance. The riddle was soon to be solved.

An occasion arose whereby Herk was called into O'Dwyer's quarters and asked to assist in effecting a rather delicate assignment. It seems that O'Dwyer had political ties in Washington. In fact, he had been previously involved in politics and the current member of the House of Representatives from his district in Queens was an intimate, a crony from a clique of indulgent souls. They had been regulars at **Skippy's Bar** where a good bit of the politics of the neighborhood was contrived. O'Dwyer was, effectively, Mortimer Brother's eye to Washington. He could usually ascertain the political agenda before even the journalistic predators.

The task he put before Herkimer had a more than incidental link to government. O'Dwyer had garnered hearsay of a man reported to be of acuity in ferreting out the schemes of not one but both political parties. The man was an independent operator who worked on consignment to corporations and organizations in the conveyance of supposedly confidential knowledge about pending legislation, a sort of spy on the legislative process. O'Dwyer reckoned that an arrangement whereby this man should work exclusively for Mortimer Brothers could reap salubrious reward. Herkimer's obvious integrity, acumen and grasp of the Spanish language had convinced O'Dwyer that he should be the one to make contact and negotiation with the gentleman, one Juan "Johnnie" Cerebino, who was of Cuban descent.

Arrangements having been made for an audience, Herk was dispatched to the D.C. to bargain with the intrepid Latino. He had contacted Arnold Schwarz, and, upon arrival, and having checked in at the hotel, Herk joined his friend at a small restaurant located back of the Capitol building in the neighborhood in which Arnold resided. They sat in a long, open room with a bar which ran the length along one side. The bar was faced by a bench along the opposite wall with narrow tables before it, set at intervals, one chair to each, making a quite compatible milieu for conversation. Arnold was already posted behind one of these tables when Herk arrived.

"It certainly is good to see you," said Herk as he took the seat opposite his friend.

Arnold smiled, looking genial about their reunion, but soon it was evident that he was not pleased with his situation.

"Washington is hell," he said. "Literally hell."

"Is it the city or your job?"

"All jobs in Washington are the same. Nothing but currying favors or calling in markers. Suckin' ass, suckin' ass, suckin' ass. And nothing ever gets done the way it should be done. Everything's done half-assed because it's all done on compromise. Almost makes me think I should be working for the Mafia. When they do something they do it all the way."

"Worse than the Mafia, hunh?" Herk was amused at his friend's unaccustomed petulance.

"You wouldn't believe it, Herk. Gossip, gossip, gossip. Everyone wants to find some scandal on someone else, something to threaten someone else with, in order to get something *they* want. I've been here four years and ..."

"Why have you stayed so long?" Herk interrupted.

"What else can I do? I don't have any other experience. That's why Washington people stay here. They move from one job to the next, doing the same thing; collecting gossip and using it to get a better paying job." Arnold shrugged as though in despair.

"Arnie," Herk said, a bit disgruntled with his old pal. "You have an MBA. That's' worth something. Come back to New York."

Arnold looked down at his hands clasped before him on the table.

"I still owe on the loan I took to get through graduate school."

"How much do you owe?":

Arnold was reluctant to tell. He looked across the room, with a vague expression.

"You can tell me," Herk said. "Maybe I can help you."

"I still owe twenty thousand dollars."

Herk looked with compassion at his friend and, with humility, said quietly, "My first bonus was that—my first year."

Herkimer, of course, financed the meal and their drinks before and after. Although Arnold made an attempt to share the cost Herk would not consider it. From that meal onward Herk determined to keep a steady pressure on Arnold and to do all he could to assist in his friend's deliverance from the hell of Washington to, at least, the purgatory of Wall Street.

"I thought it would be exciting to work in the capital," Arnold said as they bade adieu, "but these are the dullest people I've ever been around."

"We'll get you out of here," said Herk, but Arnold only shrugged hopelessly.

Next morning Herk was up early for a breakfast meeting with Señor Cerebino, a man of mid-height with smooth, immaculate hide crested by glossy, black hair, who immediately requested that Herk refer to him as Johnnie.

Herkimer, who had, in the past year, improved in his aptitude for spewing flattery promptly said, "You are famous, even in New York, Mr. Cerebino...uh, Johnnie."

Cerebino nodded his approbation to Herk's correction, then shrugged, "Well, I have become adept at my vocation."

"And how would you describe that vocation?"

"Actually, I am the only person I know who treats of the things I do. There are, of course, many influence peddlers in Washington, but I am far from that. I think of myself as a sort of watchdog of the public interest. Whenever one group begins to get too influential—even if I have helped them—I go over to another. I like to think that I help everyone to keep in balance."

Herkimer was intrigued by this guy, but there was a sensation which touched him, intrinsically, of repugnance. There was no outward symptom, no artifice in the eyes, no roguish grin to the lips; he spoke directly, seemingly without contrivance. It was, perhaps, this which put Herk on his guard. The man took pride in telling of his mastery of political intrigue. The harsh discipline of absolute probity which had been instilled in Herk by The Judge made him increasingly disillusioned with the machinations required of him in his occupation. But obedience was another of the virtues he had been taught. He would carry out, to the best of his capability, the task which he had been assigned by those to whom he owed fealty by dint of employment. He laid upon the breakfast table the proposition, devised by O'Dwyer, which would be, Herkimer avowed, quite remunerative to Johnnie Cerebino if he should decide to tie his fortunes to those of Mortimer Brothers.

"What's my cut?" asked Cerebino. "And do I get a salary and expenses?"

"I can't tell you that," said Herkimer. "That's for you to discuss with the head guys. But they did tell me I could promise that you would profit as though you were a partner in the firm. They'd like you to come to New York to discuss it with them. They'll pay your expenses, of course."

Cerebino, for the first time, looked crafty. "And why did they send *you*?"

"Porque hablo espanol."

Cerebino laughed heartily. "Afraid I would want to speak Spanish?"

"No. They thought it might seem more compatible to you if you knew we had an interest in Latin America. I'm in the department that deals in Latin America."

By noon Herk was back in the air shuttling to La Guardia with an assurance from Johnnie Cerebino that he would think seriously on the proposal and call with a decision to either come to New York or forget the deal.

Before Herk boarded the plane, however, he talked once more to Arnold Schwarz, assuring his longtime comrade that he would unearth an opportunity or two in New York. When he returned to the office in the afternoon he reported to Frank O'Dwyer his conversation with Johnnie Cerebino and also registered his mistrust of the facile Cuban.

"Me b'y," said O'Dwyer, affecting his brogue, "sure and y'er too damned honest fer this business—faith, any business. Ye should go ta seminary an' take yer orders."

"Perhaps I will," said Herkimer with a woeful countenance.

"Now, Herk," O'Dwyer dropped the brogue, "you are one of our brightest young men. We need you and men like you. We don't want to simply turn the financial world over to the women, now, do we?"

"Why not?" Herk said with a dour expression. "They're smarter than we are."

"Ms. Rosen..." (Even O'Dwyer used the proper gender title for her.) "...that's why you say that. You're trained by her and she is sharp. Sharp enough that she wouldn't pass up a chance to get Johnnie Cerebino keepin' 'is eye open fer opportunities."

He had slipped back into his brogue.

It transpired that Cerebino did come to New York and did sign a contract for one year to be Mortimer's Washington watchdog, writing into the details of the agreement, nonetheless, that he did not forfeit all rights to supply some of his previous clients with information provided he, first, pass on the details to Mortimer. Herkimer, to his dismay, was designated as the agent through whom Johnnie's tips would be conveyed.

The operation was smooth and successful. Mortimer made considerable gains for some of their big clients—and for the partners—on tips Johnnie had given them about pending legislation which would be highly beneficial to some large industries, among them two with investments in Latin America for whom our government had interceded with the Latin governments involved. The brokers bought large sums of puts on margin. In a couple of months profits had paid Cerebino's guarantee and he had earned a hearty bonus.

One morning Herk was hacking at the computer, a pastime in which he often engaged to relieve his ennui, when he made a discovery which was disconcerting. He had, only an hour before, been on the line with Cerebino who had advised him to buy shares in a mining stock, for the government had made clandestine agreement to lease the mining company a large portion of public land on which, it was known, lay an infinite tonnage of uranium ore. Herkimer appropriately alerted his superiors to place their calls. At the moment he had released this information he had also verified the price via the same computer. Now, to his consternation, he saw that the price for that stock had actually fallen dramatically. Herk smelled a rat.

He continued, on the computer, to follow the price of mining stocks into the afternoon. The price of that particular issue continued its downward slide for a time but had stabilized by the end of trading. It had, however, lost a quarter of its value from the point when he had been alerted to recommend the brokers to buy.

The following day did not improve the plight of those clients who had bought the stock. It hovered at its low, making no appearance to increase in value. Herkimer found himself in Mr. O'Dwyer's office. He had a suspicion he wished to advance.

"I think we've been conned," he said.

"What do you mean?" O'Dwyer seemed unaware of the catastrophe they had sustained.

"That mining stock," said Herk. "I think that whole story about the government lease was made up to screw us. The stock went down—by about a quarter."

"Now, me b'y, don't be takin' it so personal." The scent of alcohol wafted across the desk. "Sure an' we give it a day or so. When they announce the makin' of the lease we'll see our fortunes turn."

Herkimer, however, had already laid plans to investigate the matter. He had enlisted the aid of Arnold Schwarz. Arnold, after all, had been engaged in lobbying scams; he should be able to learn whether there was any truth in the leasing story. Late in the afternoon when the markets had closed Herk received a call from Arnold.

"I can't find anyone who knows anything about the government making any deals with a mining company," Arnold reported.

"I didn't think you would," Herk answered. "And, listen, we've got to get you out of that snake pit of corruption. Maybe both of us should think about going west. Chicago. Or Denver. I've about had it here."

Still, he was determined to unearth the truth about Cerebino's mining stock. The price had not risen. Mortimer Brothers and its clients had sustained large losses. Time had come and gone for the call payments to be made and it had been at a price far higher than the current value. Herkimer sought audience with O'Dwyer. When he was ushered into his boss's office he immediately stated his purpose.

"I want to go back down to Washington and sniff around until I find out what really happened with that mining stock."

By now O'Dwyer had been made aware of the disaster and readily gave his consent. Before departure Herk secured a second audience, this with Ms. June Rosen.

"I have a friend in Washington who is smarter than I, has an MBA from Columbia and four years working as a lobbyist in Washington. He wants to get out of that hell hole and I think he'd be a great addition to your staff. He's a fast learner."

"A Columbia guy?" Ms. Rosen was fascinated. It was just the time when the MBA theology had become the business gospel of America. "If he's got any good sense we can use him."

"You'll like him," Herk assured her.

So Herk went to Washington with two purposes. For four days he investigated not just the mining company fiasco but Cerebino's activities during the fortnight past. With the help of Arnold he held numerous luncheon chats with people who might have even an outside chance of possessing knowledge about Cerebino's activities. He also sought and gained interviews with some journalists whose bailiwick was finance. At the end of this time he had what he needed and headed back to New York accompanied by Arnold who had agreed to an interview with Ms. Rosen.

While he was in Washington he had, indeed, uncovered some scandalous information about Johnnie Cerebino. One of the contacts Herk made had informed him that Johnnie was a known associate of Eugenio Ratzaff, Washington's most notorious stock trader. From a financial reporter known for his investigative acumen he learned of the rumor that Ratzaff had made obscene profits on a certain mining stock by selling it at precisely its highest value. It didn't require a thorough knowledge of the trading business to put those two morsels of gossip together and come to the conclusion that Mortimer had been purposely finagled.

Herk informed O'Dwyer of his discovery, and it was agreed that Cerebino should be informed of the termination of his contract. Herkimer took great pleasure in being the informant. In a personal confrontation he informed the cunning Cuban that the contract was canceled with the promise of legal action if this decision were contested. Cerebino took it with aplomb and Herk was convinced that it had been Johnnie's purpose from the beginning to effect this precise outcome. He left Washington vowing never to return, transporting his friend, and soon to be associate, back to New York. When June and Arnold met it proved, instantaneously, to be a beneficent connection. June proffered employment and Arnold accepted, all within two hours. Within a month Herk's former roommate was ensconced in an apartment on the Upper West Side not four blocks distant from our matchmaker's own quarters. The confrere's were re-united, at least to the extent that they once again could make daily contact.

XI

Arnold, having been hired by June Rosen, was assigned to work for her. Indeed, June had advanced to the position of Division Head so that she had a list of regular clients and a staff of twelve reporting to her.

Herk was not altogether pleased that he had effected this change in Arnold's career. He was not satisfied with his own career, as we know, but he reckoned that perhaps, for his friend, anything might be more agreeable than the pismire heap that was Washington. As it happened Ms. Rosen developed quite an affinity for Mr. Schwarz. As you may recall Arnold was a full hand higher than our Herk; he had fine, rugged features and was, therefore, more attractive, on sight, than his diminutive friend. In fact, Ms. Rosen was stricken, and it was only work place decorum which prevented her, in the beginning, inviting Arnold to visit her living quarters of an evening. As so often happens, however, lust provoked a suspension of—nay, a downright disregard for—rules of proper deportment, and before long Arnold found himself spending more time on weekends in June Rosen's Brooklyn Heights duplex than in his own studio on Ninety-Second Street. This disturbed, somewhat, Herkimer's principles of propriety, but being fully aware of the age of incontinence in which he lived, he was able to forgive his friend and maintain a comradeship, though he seldom spoke to Arnold of Ms. Rosen who, since she was several years the elder, he considered the more culpable.

This liaison was, indeed, to prove to his advantage for a remarkable new episode was to occur in his life. He was now determined that he should make a change in employment. What that should be he was not at all certain, but he was not content arranging mergers and acquisitions for Mortimer Brothers. Although he had been in the money game for five years and was earning at a rate in the six figure category with a bonus which doubled his salary at year's end, he decided he would consult a career advisor and made an appointment to spend five hundred dollars on a three day course, given by a man advertised as Professor Lang, at the Vocational Institute of America. It was hardly even a three day course. It extended over three days, but the first day consisted of a one hour lecture by Professor Lang followed by a fifteen minute interview with a young man who pried into Herk's past to discover his fields of interest. The second day consisted of a one hour test to ascertain his aptitude in a number of pursuits, and on the third day, which might be postponed as much as a week succeeding the test, there was an interview of perhaps twenty minutes with the good Professor during which the aptitudes revealed on the test were discussed and an executive search company—which Herk suspected had some ties to the Institute—was recommended to assist the client in landing a job in the field of his/her interest.

It was necessary that Herk, for these sessions, transport himself to Mid-town from Wall Street, so he arranged to attend evening sessions of the "course." The lecture proved of little interest to Herk since it told him things that seemed necessary to any job search—that one should engage in an enterprise holding some inherent interest which arose from his life experience and which would motivate him to put forth great effort toward success. In the interview afterwards he was presented with a folder which gave instructions on preparation for the examination. The exam was simple and also predictable and Herk finished it in twenty minutes. It was an occurrence during this third visit to Mid-town which would have enduring effect on his life, and it was only tangentially associated with the Institute.

As he pushed open the glass door to the Institute lobby, on the twenty-fourth floor of 1080 Avenue of the Americas, his eye was assailed with a vision. He blinked at the strength of his shock, but when his sight returned to normal his original surprise was verified: the vision moved, turned its head and gazed directly into his face; a smile stretched its cheeks and Herkimer stumbled into the lobby, reached down to the low table between the waiting room chairs to steady himself and gaped into the fair countenance of his secret, immortal beloved, Deeana Wallis.

"Herkimer!" she cried and, jumping from the chair she sat in, Deeana kissed him.

It was a quick buss but it fell directly on his lips. Astounded, Herk at length found his voice. "Deeana! Deeana!" He smiled so broadly his cheeks ached.

For a moment both simply stood and stared, one at the other, but then Herk could no longer suppress his longing and took the beauteous lady securely into his embrace, the supple curves of her torso pressed solidly against his firmer frame. She submitted as readily as he clutched.

After a few silent seconds Deeana began to mutter softly, "Herkie, Herkie, my dearest Herkie."

At this point the receptionist at the desk pronounced a loud, "Ar-r-umph!" as though to flush her gullet, and the two re-united friends separated, Deeana resuming her seat.

"Did you have an appointment?" the receptionist asked of Herkimer.

"Oh, yeah," he said, smiling at her and her perplexity. "I'm here to see some councilor for a report on my test. I'm Herkimer Hampton."

As the receptionist wrote his name on a pad he turned back to Deeana.

"What are you doing here?" he asked.

"Same thing you are, I presume. Only I haven't yet taken any test," she smiled. "I'm here to find out about it."

"I thought you'd be happy teaching English," he said taking a chair next to her.

"I have been," she said, "but it's not a long term career. It gets old. I mean, it's not like teaching literature or history. It gets old fast." She reached across the space between them and put her hand on his. "But how about you? Why are you here?"

"Well," he was hesitant to express his true sentiments, "I just have a feeling I may be in the wrong business."

She smiled as though she comprehended. "Don't like the money business, hunh?"

"You know me," he said quietly. "Just a simple country boy. I guess the pressure gets to me."

"You're too damned honest for them."

He was quizzical. "How do you know about it?"

"One of my brothers is in the 'big game' back in Minneapolis. All they talk about is how they've screwed someone."

"In Minnesota?"

"Well, they don't come right out and say it but you get the idea that's what it's all about."

They were interrupted by the receptionist who called both of them to their interviews.

"Listen," Herk said, taking Deeana's hand as they crossed the opening to the interior hallway, "let's have dinner after. Please, please!"

"Love to," she said. "Whoever finishes first will wait out here."

And so it was the two college companions were re-united.

"How did yours go?" she asked as they met in the Institute lobby.

"I'll tell you about it," he grinned as they headed out toward the elevator. "First, where shall we go to eat?"

"I don't know New York. You'll have to pick."

"Okay, we'll go over to La Veranda. It's nearby." He looked down at his watch. "It's almost eight o'clock. The theater crowd will have left. We shouldn't have any trouble getting a table."

As they walked the few blocks to the restaurant Herkimer decided to tell her of his experience with the job councilor.

"He told me my tests showed I would do very well on Wall Street—as a trader or in mergers and acquisitions." He was grinning broadly.

Deeana smiled, too. "Isn't that what you're doing?"

"Of course it is."

"What did you tell him?"

"I told him that I had been hoping to find another line of work which wasn't quite so high-pressure, something that gave me a bit more free time."

They had arrived at the restaurant and, as they approached the maitre'd, Deeana looked approvingly at the ambiance: walls of ivory, ornamented at intervals by paintings of delicate good taste, table cloths of immaculate white, set with sparkling crystal goblets.

"This is hardly the kind of place we were used to eating in," she said, raising her eyebrows.

"That's one thing about this job I have. I make good money. Let's me eat in places like this."

"Then why would you want to change?"

He looked at her as though injured.

"I thought you knew me better than that."

"Well, I don't really know anything about your job, do I. I don't know anything about Wall Street—or any other business it seems." She sighed. "My interview was a disaster."

Herk was truly concerned, now, and more than slightly angered at this so-called Institute.

"What did they tell you?" he asked, the gall evident in his voice.

"They advised me to go back to graduate school and get an MBA. But I'm supposed to show up tomorrow for the lecture."

"Your experience in China should be a big plus in a lot of businesses."

"Oh yeah, they said if I had an MBA my language skills would be of great value."

"Jesus!" Herk exclaimed. "I went to business school for a semester and I learned more in the first month on the job than I did in that damned place. What's more, after I'd been on the job for a year they had me teaching the MBA's they hired what to do. They didn't know how to act in the business world any more than I did when I started. The only difference was their arrogance. They thought they knew it all. I had to be kind of tough on some of them."

"Not everyone's as smart as you, my dear Herkie," she said grinning across the table at him.

This made him self-conscious; he decided it was time to order food and signaled the waiter, who stood only a table away.

He had been correct in assuming that the early theater crowd had come and gone, and so they received prompt and swift service.

As they sipped their wine they delved into their activities of the five years since they had been college mates. Deeana had spent the first three of those in China teaching English, of course, but also learning to speak Chinese.

"The Chinese people were so nice to me," she said. "They did everything they could to help me feel comfortable."

"You didn't see any of the repression we read about over here?"

"No. But then I didn't have to deal with the bureaucrats. My bosses did that."

"And the last two years? Where were you then?"

"India," she said, making a wry face.

"And is that why you decided to quit?"

"Well, I got sick."

"Oh, my God."

"Yeah," she said. "It's a filthy country, crawling with dirty people. And they don't like us."

"Does anyone like us?"

"The Chinese people," she said. "The ordinary people and, of course, a lot of them have relatives here."

He reached out and took her hand. "And how are you now?"

"I'm okay," she said without ardor. "I still take medicine for it, though."

"And that's why you're looking for a different kind of job?"

"Not really. I was getting bored teaching English, as I said. I thought maybe I could do something more interesting, something that would help me to grow."

"I would guess that those years in China helped you grow a lot. Remember, I took Chinese history with Professor Chan. I have great admiration for their culture. According to Chan they still follow most of the teachings of Lao Tzu. The Tao is like their bible."

"Except for the Buddhists, and even they embrace much of the wisdom of the Tao," she said.

"Hell," he said, shrugging, "it's all the same, isn't it? If you've ever read Joseph Campbell—he convinced me. All humans have a burning need for some spiritual answer, something beyond the supposed certainty of science, of what we can observe. We want a spiritual answer."

She was grinning broadly, enjoying this. "And is there one?"

"Only for the 'true believer'."

"And are you one?"

"Afraid not."

"And what *do* you believe?"

He looked at her, quizzically, for a moment before answering, then said, "In order to best describe my belief I must paraphrase the French adage about change. The only certainty is un-certainty."

"Very good," she smiled. "I see you have not abandoned your skeptical attitude."

"Then you approve?"

"Very much so. People who can't question cant simply can't make progress."

"And still I believe there is more than the empirical, more than we know or probably ever can know, something we can only feel." He smiled at her. "Is that nuts or what?"

"Not so crazy. Even up into the nineteenth century most philosophers believed in God. And even Nietzsche—you can tell when he writes that 'God is dead' in **Thus Spake Zarathustra**—you can tell he's reluctant, that he wishes it weren't so."

The appetizers came, and while they ate they continued the kind of catch-up conversation common to old friends who haven't been in touch for a long period, especially those as intimate as were these two. Upon consummation of the meal Herkimer escorted Deeana to The Barbizon Plaza, a hotel on the East side where she was registered. Before embarking by cab for his apartment on the West side he made certain that she had his telephone number, that he had that of the hotel, and they made plans to meet on the following evening after she had gone to the lecture by Professor Lang.

Before parting he said to her, "You don't have to stay in this hotel. I have a big, two bedroom apartment across town now. You could stay there with me—in your own bedroom—as long as you'd like."

"Oh," she said. "Let me think about that." But next evening when he went to meet her at the Institute she had her luggage with her, a large suitcase, and they promptly contacted a cab to take them to his abode.

They were quite proper in their living arrangement. Herk had the two bedrooms and in one, which he used as his home office, where his computer was ensconced, there was a day bed. He insisted that he should use this and Deeana should sleep in his bed. She made proper protest but he was insistent, and, so, that was the arrangement by which they lived while she was in New York.

It was on this second evening they were together that she made inquiry which he had been perplexed she had not made earlier.

"And what about Arnold?" she asked him as they supped at a bistro near his apartment.

Herk found it a bit awkward to give his reply. It was hard to imagine that perhaps Deeana did not feel about Arnold as she had five or six years before, and Herk was loathe to be the bearer of the news that her once boy-friend had found a new playmate.

"Oh," he said, beginning with a flourish. "Arnold is just fine. He works at the same place I do."

"Really." she said, with a quizzical look. "How nice for both of you. And where does he live?":

"Well," it was becoming more difficult, "he...well, he lives over in Brooklyn."

"Brooklyn? I don't think I've ever known anyone who lived in Brooklyn," her eyes had a special vivacity. "And does he have a girl friend?"

"Well...sort of. I mean, yeah, he does. She's a bit older than he—she used to be my boss at Mortimer. Now he's working for her."

"And living with her," Deeana grinned.

"What...?" Herk was flustered. How did she know?

"Come on. That's what people do these days. And why else would he live in Brooklyn?" She seemed unduly amused.

"True," Herk smiled. "All you say is true. He is living over in Brooklyn with Ms. June Rosen, an extremely intelligent and able Wall Street dealer."

"Good," Deeana was delighted. "I'd hoped he had someone. He's a nice boy. He needs a woman."

"And...?" Herk was hesitant. "What about you? Do you have a boy friend—a nice Chinaman...or Indian?" He smiled to show it was a tease.

"No," she said with a sigh. "I've only ever loved one guy."

"Oh, I'm sorry." Herk assumed she referred to Arnold.

"Why are you sorry? He's still available," she was enjoying the dialogue more than he.

"Back home—in Minnesota?"

"No. Right here."

"In New York?" He was amazed.

"Right here! Here in this restaurant." She beamed across the table at him.

As the meaning of what she said became manifest his face took on an expression of confusion. He looked closely into her eyes for a clue to her intent. Was she joking?

"Yes," she said with simple sincerely. "You. It's always been you. I hung around with Arnold so I could be near you, because you—you sweet, dear thing—were too modest to profess your love, which I, nonetheless, felt. In fact," she added, "I believe I still do."

Herkimer found it necessary to look away, to place his hand to his brow and squeeze away the emotion which brimmed moist in his eyes. She said no more, and, after a moment, he looked once again to her with a smile beneath his wet cheeks.

"Oh, God," he said. "I could never have believed that."

"Now you have to," she said, "because it's true—isn't it?"

"Oh, yes. Yes. I've always loved you. It's just that I could never...well, I never imagined you thought of me as...well, anything more than just a friend, a special friend, yes, but not more."

And so it was, toward the end of the ninth decade of our Twentieth Century, Herkimer Hartland Hampton did plight his troth to Deeana Spencer Wallis. They would decide to marry, without lavish ceremony. They took their oaths in a small Protestant church on the West Side, before a modest assemblage of friends from their secondary schools as well as from Occom, and a certain number of relatives. Deeana's parents came from Minnesota, and The Judge came out from Iowa to see his only heir joined in Holy matrimony in the Big Apple.

It was a joyous occasion. Cousin Joe and Judge Hampton were re-united after many years of separation, and a score or more stories of the vicissitudes of youth in the hills of Southern Iowa passed unchallenged as to veracity. Even Cousin Sylvia found the Wallis family of acceptable breeding, and everyone was pleased, with the exception of Arnold who served as best man. He had never foreseen this result and, as Herk ascertained, he was at this moment somewhat discontent in his relationship with Ms Rosen. Arnold tried to maintain a jolly attitude, but Herk could see that it was affected.

During the reception held, through the generosity of Cousin Joe, at the Racquet Club, Deeana took Arnold aside and, struggling to maintain total honesty, assured him that the threesome would maintain their previous close attachment; that he, Arnold, would always be welcome at the Hampton residence.

And so it was that Herkimer embarked on a new episode of life as a married man.

XII

Marriage for Herkimer and Deeana did not prove to be the perfect answer to their dreams and desires, but as that ancient institution is practiced at the end of the second millennium AD, theirs would be called good. They each learned to make most of the concessions necessary for humans of the opposing species to dwell together in relative harmony.

While Herk had been restless in his chosen vocation he saw that, in order to maintain his wife according to the custom in which she had been nurtured, he would needs deliver the kind of elevated income to which he, himself, had become accustomed.

It was not necessary, however, that he continue at Mortimer Brothers. The financial world was known for instability; that he had been more than five years in one place was unusual. It was also true that having Arnold in the same office was a bit difficult. They maintained a firm friendship and Arnold dined with Herk and Deeana on occasion but Herk could not rid himself of a guilt he felt at having, in his view, taken away Arnold's lady love. And so, after a year of marriage, Herkimer began to send out his resume. Deeana, upon taking the vows, had not changed her profession but found employment with Berlitz in New York City.

After a three month search Herk found a position with another Wall Street firm, Gunther Investment, a subsidiary of Gunther, Marcus and Schapp, known generally as The GMS Group. Gunther Investment was the mergers and acquisitions branch.

Herk's new salary was fifty percent higher than his previous and he had considerably better perquisites, one being a liberal expense account which would allow him, if he were so disposed, to take friends to lunch or dinner under the guise that they were prospective clients, and, the first year after joining them, he was not surprised that his year end bonus actually exceeded his salary by twenty percent.

So it was that the following four years were quite remunerative to Herk and Deeana. During this period Herk found it judicious to invest in the stock market. He had good advisors in GMS who showed him how to turn the great plummet of the market in 1987 into a healthy profit. Our couple entered the final decade of the Century with something more than a million dollars on their ledger, a sizable amount it would seem, yet only what was needed, in these times, to assure their survival were they to find themselves without other means.

As they entered the decade of the Nineties Herk decided that he would prefer to pursue an endeavor which might bear some beneficial fruit for future generations. He and Deeana had now passed the catalytic age of thirty and, in the previous year, she had produced, with his help, a beautiful female offspring. It was perhaps this blessed event which gave impetus to Herk's latest ambition to help effectuate a more benign culture. Even while in college he had been aware of the healthy discourse on the dangers of the pollution of our soil and atmosphere by the profligate expansion of production and consumption.

"Honey," he said to Deeana one evening after they had placed the baby in her crib, "I've been thinking about the future, not just ours but Penelope's." For that was the name they had bestowed upon the tiny girl. "Rather than just make money—and mostly for other people—I'd rather be doing something that would be good for society."

"That's admirable," said his spouse. "Like what?"

"Oh, something that has to do with the environment, ecology. Maybe work for a waste disposal company. Any outfit that's trying to reduce pollution."

And so with Deeana's support he began his search for a meaningful lifetime endeavor. It took him a year to identify two possibilities. During that time he worked harder than ever at GMS because he did not want anyone, most importantly himself, to feel he had, in any way, been derelict in his duties when the time came to announce his intent to alter course. Because of his increased attention to duty he was rewarded, at year's end, with his largest bonus ever— close to half a million dollars which, as he remarked to Deeana, when invested properly along with his other assets would render them practically immune to any future episode of ill fortune. They could subsist even during intervals of unemployment.

Also, during that one year period he found, at NYU, an evening class in ecology and enrolled, so that when the time came to announce his career change he had more than a dilettante's knowledge of his subject.

After much investigation he had limited his choice to two companies, each with quite different aims than the other. One sought simply to see to the healthful disposal of waste, especially that which could pollute the land and waters. The other sought, through development of a new form of energy called cold fusion, to eliminate, totally, the use of fossil fuel.

After much deliberation he decided to go with the waste. It was something he understood more easily—that is, he knew what constituted waste for the most part. Cold fusion was something he did not fully grasp though it had been explained to him, shown to him, by the company producing the machines which induced it, and he had read about it in his night course at NYU. It required a degree in physics to be totally proficient, Herk reasoned, and so he decided on the simple waste disposal position. Still, if he could believe everything told him and demonstrated by the cold fusion company, that seemed the only discovery on the horizon which could promise redemption of our planet.

It might seem unlikely that a company engaged in waste disposal would find attractive a Wall Street hustler, but his entrance position was that of a salesman, a pursuit in which he felt somewhat at home, for that was, in effect, what he had been doing all his years with Mortimer and GMS.

The name of the company which provided Herk's employment was prophetic: World Without End, shortened in general reference to WWE, often referred to simply as "we." The man to whom Herk reported had the title Director of Sales and Marketing, a position, Herk was aware, that every company, even one engaged in trash, must have in these latter days of the century. The man's name was Wolfe Hucksburgh. He was of German descent and, while draconian in Teutonic fashion, not without a dry sense of humor.

"I should think," Herk remarked to Hucksburgh in the early days of his employment, "that a waste disposal firm would need very little promotion. Everyone has to dispose of trash."

"Yes," said Hucksburgh, "most communities now have their own disposal companies. We are going to make it more efficient. We will expand into many locales. Some day in the not too distant future—because of our advanced technology—we will be one of the few disposal companies in the country, perhaps the only disposal company in the country. We will—you might say— dispose of all the others."

Hucksburgh smiled at this little pun but Herk did not see the humor.

"What about anti-trust laws?" Herk asked.

"There will be no need to worry, for everyone will trust in us."

It was not an auspicious beginning for Herkimer. He had thought he was getting into an endeavor dedicated to making the environment benign. But, after all, he told himself, it is a business and, like all business, the purpose is to make money.

His first assignment was to be enlightening. It seems that WWE had made a contract with the inventors of the cold fusion apparatus, the same people for whom Herk had considered working, and so he would be selling this machine which could, if it did as promised, reduce all waste to nothing more than the various atoms of its composition. Hucksburgh assured Herk that WWE now held exclusive patent on this modern marvel. This, of course, surprised Herkimer since he had been in such recent contact with the makers and had heard nothing of an exclusive arrangement with any other company.

Herk, however, decided that this contract must have been effected quite recently and, so, did not question further his assignment to spread the word, to sell this marvelous machine abroad. The price of each was rather lofty, one might say astronomical. The leasing of even the smaller of two available sizes was five hundred and fifty thousand dollars per year and the outright purchase almost three times that. The sale of only a few would bring a sound profit to the company, and Herk figured that, with the promise it held, he might find success.

Herk's first assignment, then, was to travel westward and cajole the disposal bureaucrats of Minneapolis into the use of WWE's "Disposal Unit of the 21st Century." It was not to be an easy sale.

The authorities in Minneapolis found it difficult to understand his description of total disappearance of waste. It took all of Herk's minimal powers of locution to explain to them what happened to waste when subjected to the powers of the cold fusion machine.

"Just as the hot fusion of atomic or hydrogen bombs released atoms of U-235 as destructive energy," he attempted to explain, "the cold fusion machine releases atoms in waste as pure non-energy."

It didn't even make much sense to him but he persisted in his attempt at explanation. These atoms, he continued, would simply evaporate into the atmosphere, actually cleaning the air by attracting other particles of pollution and rendering them harmless.

There were four men in the group to whom he presented his proposition, and all found it difficult to ingest this description. But Herk had come well prepared. He had brought along a video which had been used to educate him to the wonders of cold fusion. In it they saw the sewage from a giant football stadium pour out and through an open conduit into a WWE cold fusion machine. Beyond the machine was a large greenhouse into which the products, both air and water, from the WWE machine were ejected. In the soil of the atrium grew beautiful arbors of grape, patches of corn and other vegetables. The video included a narrative which proclaimed the purity of the air, the earth and the water which ran from the conduit into rivulets of irrigation between the rows of plants. A man appeared. He picked some grapes and savored them, then washed them down with a cup of water he drew directly from the gushing conduit which was connected to the WWE machine.

"This," said Herkimer in his guileless candor, "convinced me. For I confess that, at first, I had serious doubts."

"Have you actually seen this done—personally?" asked one of the bureaucrats.

"I have done it," Herk proclaimed, for this, indeed, had been a part of his training. "I actually tasted the water."

One, a large man with muffin cheeks and blonde hair which was unable or unwilling to stay at rest above his broad brow, grinned wickedly and said, "So you had to learn to eat shit...!"

The other three voiced their pleasure at this salacious remark with loud hee-haws.

"But," said the one who had announced himself as Dean Wilkie, City Treasurer, who was sitting in a deep chair, looking almost dwarfish next to his companions and with a paucity of hair to match his size, "this is human sewage you've used to demonstrate your machine. Our big problem is industrial waste, the crap that comes out of all the factories along the river. It can pollute the river and, if we're not careful, our drinking water. We already add far too much chlorine to it. Everybody tells us our water tastes awful."

At this Herkimer had a sudden moment of lucidity but spoke as though what he said were no more than standard procedure. "Why don't you pass a law which requires all factories to make all waste as clean as our machines can make it?"

The small, hairless man raised his brows and pursed his lips, looking to each of his fellows in turn. Each returned his expression of revelation.

"Tell us again, Mr. Hartland," said Shorty, "your company both leases <u>and</u> sells these machines?"

"Yes, Sir."

"And the price? I don't believe you told us how much this machine would cost to buy," said Wilkie whose austere demeanor intimidated Herkimer.

"Well, Sir," Herk said, swallowing his agitation, "we have two sizes, two types actually. There is the large one to be used by regional disposal systems and there is the individual factory size..." He paused, giving them an opportunity to choose.

"I think we might consider the individual factory size if we were to follow your suggestion, don't you?" said the depilated Shorty with irony.

"We lease that one for five fifty a year."

"Five dollars and fifty cents?" Extreme irony.

Even Herk smiled. "Five hundred and fifty thousand dollars."

"And it sells for ...?"

"Around a million and a half." Herk had some trouble getting this out; it seemed such a huge amount to him. But the four listeners did not seem intimidated. Wilkie simply nodded to his three associates.

The large blonde actually laughed. "A nominal fee," he said and the two who had, heretofore, been expressionless and unresponsive now actually laughed. These two flunkies—for that is how Herk perceived them—were both of medium height and looked almost clones except for their complexions, one ruddy and dissipated, the other flat and sallow.

"Well," said Shorty, arising from his chair, "we will, of course, think it over." And, turning to one of the larger men, added, "You have this gentleman's card I assume."

"I'll get it," said Hefty. And with that the small man with his two other associates left the room.

"You really know what you're tryin' to sell?" Hefty said, not a question so much as a challenge.

"Yes," said Herkimer, somewhat peeved now. "We're selling a cleaner environment, perhaps even something to help save the Earth for future generations."

"You're one of those, hunh?" said Hefty. "Well, gimme one of your cards and we'll let you know. We're just tryin' to run a city and we gotta watch our budget."

Herkimer extracted one of his business cards and handed it to Hefty who took it peremptorily, turned toward the door and said, "We'll let you know."

Herk followed Hefty from the room but was left to track his own way from the city administration building. He went directly to the airport and boarded the plane back to New York, feeling rather despondent that his first call in his new career had apparently failed.

His spirits were lifted, however, as he gazed from the aircraft down at the fruitful fields of the Mid-west over which they passed in the early minutes of the flight. It was late spring and he looked down on the orderly layout of land below. It was arranged in perfect squares, some still dark from the plow, crossed by thin, straight rows where the corn had just begun to sprout. The fields were divided, at intervals, by curving lines of trees where, he knew, ran the multitude of creeks and rivers which drained the verdant plain. Home, he thought. Perhaps this is where I belong.

It was but three days later that he received a call from Wilkie. An assistant in the sales department took the call, then announced to Herk, "It's Dean Wilkie, Treasurer of the city of Minneapolis. He wants to speak to you.".

"Mr. Hartland?" came a voice which seemed straight from the person's sinus cavities. "This is Dean Wilkie in Minneapolis."

"Oh, yes Sir..." The call was unexpected.

"We would like to discuss the...uh...thing you told us about at further length, perhaps with your CEO...or...uh, your President."

"Oh! Well...uh...I suppose I could arrange that," Herk was perplexed. Did this kind talk only with the top guy?

"Would you please." It wasn't a question from Small Nasal but a request, almost a demand. "Have your CEO call me, would you." And the connection was immediately broken.

Herk was more than slightly intimidated. He had never met the President who was also the CEO of WWE. Herk had seen the Big Man but a few times. On one occasion, upon working late, Herk mounted the elevator to find that The Chief, whose name was Will Dewar, had boarded from the floor above. When the younger man entered Dewar gave a perfunctory nod and was silent until they had descended to the lobby, at which point, when Herk stepped aside to permit his exit, he grunted a "Thank you" and hurried out to the street where a long, obscene-looking limousine awaited him.

Dewar, whose title alone was fearful, was also a man of threatening demeanor. He was tall and spare; he walked with a hauteur which discouraged any casual greeting one might contemplate extending in simple congeniality; he carried a perpetual expression of serious intent as though in constant contemplation of the immediate future.

Herk was not alone in his trepidation of the Boss, and so it was with diffidence that he approached his immediate supervisor, Wolfe Hucksburgh.

"Sir," he said while usually he would address Hucksburgh as Wolfe, "those officials in Minneapolis I visited last week have called me and asked that they be allowed to speak directly to our President. Is that a possibility?"

"What do they want to talk about?" asked Hucksburgh.

"I don't know exactly, but they seemed to be interested in my idea."

"What was your idea?"

"I suggested that maybe they should pass a law which required all the manufacturing plants in Minneapolis to clean up absolutely—the kind of clean only our machines can deliver."

Hucksburgh raised his brows, pursed his lips and said nothing for a full thirty seconds, making Herk wonder what error he had committed. But then Hucksburgh affected a smile. "You told them they should require <u>all</u> manufacturers to produce the kind of clean waste only our machines can deliver?"

"Just in Minneapolis."

Hucksburgh actually laughed. "That's quite a number of plants I'd imagine." Then, after a moment, he added, "I wonder if they could legally make everyone purchase our machine?"

"No, I don't suppose they could. But they could set the environmental standards so high that only our machines could do the job," answered Herkimer.

"Hucksburgh leered with obvious avaricious import. "And he called you back just now?"

"Yes," said Herk, "but he asked to talk only to our President."

"Well, with what you've told me I think I can arrange that."

"I thought perhaps..." Herk was about to suggest that he, himself, should convey the message to the Chief but immediately discarded the idea. He was already feeling a distaste for his new career.

"You thought what?" Hucksburgh had guessed Herk's intent and gave him a nasty glare.

"Nothing," Herk said. "I just thought you might want me to give you a more complete account of my meeting with them..."

"That won't be necessary until after I see what the boss says."

Herk was never again called to the discussions. Hucksburgh did have the courtesy to congratulate him, a couple of days after their discussion, on his idea to make it a legal necessity for plants to maintain a level of purity which could be reached only by the use of cold fusion machines. Three months hence he heard, via office gossip, that WWE had sold no fewer than six cold fusion disposal engines to the industries in Minneapolis, the first breakthrough which would allow the company to embark on major expansion.

Herkimer's initial reaction was to approach Hucksburgh for verification, but, having learned that his brash actions often proved to be errors, he refrained until a time two days later when he was in Hucksburgh's office to be informed about some more recent negotiations. There were two other staff members in the meeting and Herk waited until they had been dismissed. He made it a point to be the last to leave and, when he was near the door, turned to his supervisor and asked casually, "Say, what ever happened in Minneapolis?"

"Oh," said Hucksburgh, "we made the deal. And a good one it was. Sold several machines." Herkimer perceived that he was being dismissed with this curt answer, but as he passed through the doorway Hucksburgh added, "That idea about passing a law with higher standards—that was a good one. We might use that on other locales. The Chief was pleased."

"Thanks," Herk said, with what drollery he could muster, and stepped into the hall. He did not ask whether the Chief had been informed that it was his idea for he feared he knew the answer.

During the following twelve months Herk was dispatched to no fewer than twenty cities across the continent to establish contact with, in some instances, the city bureaucrats and, in others, with managers at leading waste disposal companies. His was always initial contact; he was never called upon, indeed allowed, to follow up and complete any contracts, though he became aware, through office gossip, that several had been consummated.

Then, one morning as he prepared for the day, completing his usual ablutions, he heard via NPR News of the mysterious eruption of an epidemic among the burghers of Minneapolis and St. Paul. At first he felt only compassion for the victims—it was thought to be typhoid fever—but, as the day progressed and he ruminated on the plight of the afflicted, his pity turned to anger. For, among the items in the news surrounding the tragedy was the conjecture that the problem might be traced to factory waste, for all of the cases reported lay along the Mississippi River in the vicinity of the main production sites of the City. There, in a couple of the poorer neighborhoods, were the dwellings of the individuals afflicted.

Herkimer was highly perplexed. Had he been misinformed about the sale of the WWE machines? Had the machines failed in their promise? The questions and doubts so plagued his thoughts that he was compelled to make bold and lay the situation before his superior. After agonizing for several days he sought audience with Hucksburgh. The meeting did not augur to Herk's benefit. It was, in fact, a calamity.

"I wanted to ask you," Herk began, "if you had heard—or read—about the epidemic of typhoid which has erupted in Minneapolis."

Hucksburgh pursed his lips, shrugged and shook his head. "I don't follow the news much."

"Well, there's a terrible outbreak of typhoid fever in Minneapolis and most of the cases reported are amongst people who live along the river where most of the industry is located. They think the pollution of the Mississippi and it's tributaries by those industries might be the cause."

"So...?" Hucksburgh's one syllable response was in the form of a question.

"I thought all those factories had our disposal units in them."

"All of them? No way!" Hucksburgh scoffed.

"But I thought they passed a law. They had to have them—or at least ones that did the same job as ours."

Hucksburgh grinned slyly. "Maybe some other guys fooled 'em."

This remark was perhaps the true indication of Wolfe Hucksburgh's intellect, for had he not made suggestion of duplicity the possibility might never have occurred to Herkimer. Now, as he left the superior's office the notion dawned on him that, yes, there may have been some deceit perpetrated by none other than his own associates, the powers who directed World Without End.

As he pondered this possibility over the remaining hours of the day he became acutely agitated; he found he could focus his mind on nothing else. When he arrived, that evening, at his apartment, Deeana promptly perceived his distraction. He had been home but minutes when she remarked, "You seem preoccupied; you've scarcely noticed Penelope."

The offspring, now a conversant little girl, kept her keen eyes fixed upon Papa when they sat for their meal, as though in perception of his troubled mind. He turned his gaze to her, saw the concern in her face and, finally, smiled.

"Don't worry, Baby," he said, affecting a jollity he did not feel, "it's nothing Papa can't fix."

Seeing the pleasantry in his face she beamed at him. "Will Papa read to me?" she asked.

This was a habit they had formed; whenever he was home early enough he tucked her into her bed, then sat beside her and regaled her with tales of Dr. Seuss, Pooh Bear, or Toady and Mole. So when they had cleaned the dining table, bathed her diminutive figure and he had tucked the blankets about her, he sat and read "Green Eggs and Ham" to her delight and, for the first time in that inauspicious day, to his.

His feelings were further ameliorated by a conversation initiated by the child.

"Papa," she asked, "what is that sword in your closset—what's it for?"

He had not considered his heirloom weapon for several years and he immediately smiled on the little girl.

"It's for nothing, sweetheart. That is a priceless asset. It belonged to your great, great grandfather. He carried it in the Civil War."

"Sybil war? Is that like my friend Sybil?"

He laughed. "No sweetie. The Civil War—" he pronounced it very clearly—"was a terrible war between two factions in our own United States. A contest between those who thought they could establish their own separate country with rules to permit slavery and those who thought that our Republic should remain united, as it had been founded, but without the oppressive institution of slavery."

"What's slavery?"

"That's when one person, by law, owns another person—just as you own a doll."

"I don't understand."

"Well, your doll is not a live person. It doesn't have a mind, doesn't think or feel as you do. It can't move on its own. It has to go where you want it to go. You wouldn't want to make a real person have to do just what you said, to do your work for you without even being paid for it."

"Are there people who do that?"

"Not anymore. Not in this country. And that's because people like your great, great grandfather fought in the Civil War to make sure everyone is free to work for money and to leave a job whenever they want to—as I did when I moved from one company to another."

Herk tucked the covers under the cherub's chin and leaned to kiss her.

"I think slavery is awful," said Penelope.

"It is, sweetheart. It is." And he placed a loving buss upon her cheek and left her to her repose.

Upon return to the living chamber he found Deeana awaiting an account of his day and the cause of his disquiet. She sat resolutely on the divan, her arms folded, looking up into his face, which had brightened considerably.

"So," she said, "are you going to fill me in?"

He sighed as he sat in the arm chair facing her. "This world is full of evil," he said, "and I believe I have, once again, stumbled over it."

She motioned for him to join her on the divan and, when he responded positively, she took his hand in hers. "Okay. Let's have it."

"Well," he began, sighing once more, "I think these guys I'm working for are not entirely honest."

"What did they do to you?"

"It's not anything they did to me. It may be what I have done to some people—on their behalf."

She squeezed his hand more tightly and looked into his face, but he turned away.

"I may have caused a whole lot of people to be poisoned," he said.

Now she smiled, even chuckled, for she knew his propensity for drama.

"It's not a joke," he continued. "You know those disposal machines I've told you about? Well, they may not be all our wonderful 'executives' say they are."

"How's that?"

"You know I went to Minneapolis about a year ago and told the city officials all about our 'wonderful machine.' They talked a bunch of factories—they actually passed a law, I think—to make them buy those machines."

"How could they pass a law like that?" Deeana interrupted.

"It was a law raising the standards for pure air and water and ..."

"And who was to do the testing to ascertain the levels from the factories?"

"Oh!" Her question prompted the realization of another possibility which he now pondered in silence.

"Herkie dear?" She prodded a response.

"I don't really know. In fact, I now have doubts that they intended any stricter standards at all. It is just possible ..." he continued his rumination, "... it is possible that it was all a sham, that they took my idea and used it for fraudulent purposes."

For several minutes he remained in thought while Deeana, feeling his distraction, stroked his arm tenderly.

"Sweetheart." he said at length, "I think I have got myself into an untenable position. But, by God, I aim to get out of it. I won't go down easily and, some way, I'll see that the truth is out and that justice is done."

XIII

On this evening, which was to prove auspicious in the life of Herkimer Hartland Hampton, before retiring, he looked in upon his sleeping cherub, bundled to the chin in her downy quilt. She was serene, still and so beautiful he made more resolute his decision to do whatever was within his capacity to help assure the small angel and those of her generation a more benign environment, even if he had to fight a small civil war of his own. For the first time in his maturity he knelt beside Penelope's bed, knees to the floor and elbows on the mattress, hands clasped before his face and entreated his Father in Heaven.

"Dear God," he said softly, "please give me the strength, wisdom and capability to get to the bottom of this travesty and help set things right, for the health and welfare of our children—children of all the world—depends on our making clean and safe the beauty and beneficence of Thy nature. Amen."

Herk did not immediately perceive a wise course of action. Should he remain at WWE and proceed, from the inside, to discover the cause of this tragedy, or should he resign and broadcast his motives to those in public life who had set their goals at policing the cleanliness of our environment? Next morning at the breakfast table he outlined what he thought were his options and sought his spouse's advise.

"You can't be forthright with this group. If you quit and start looking into the operation from outside they'll probably find out what you're doing and hide their nefarious activities even more completely," she said, with energy, for she had become quite as indignant as he. "You'd best keep working there and, from the inside, look for clues as to how they're effecting this scam."

"Yeah," said Herk, grinning wickedly. "You're right—as usual. I may not find anything. I may be all wrong, but I just have a feeling that that guy Dewar is not honest. I think he'd trade in his own kid for a bunch of money. And Hucksburgh? I don't think anyone I worked with on Wall Street was as slimy as he is." He shook his head, distraught now. "Why did I ever start working for these guys?"

"Because," she said, placing her hand on his, "you thought you could help society. And maybe now you will be able to do so regardless of these S.O.B.'s, whether it's their fault of not."

From his office that morning he phoned his friend, Arnold Schwarz, and inquired after a lunch date for that day. When Arnold said he could not oblige on that particular day Herk asked if—since Arnold had, by now, returned to his apartment in Yuppieville, the Upper West Side—they might meet in the bar of a restaurant in that neighborhood. On this Arnold agreed.

The rendezvous took place at **Saki's**, a neat though small establishment, at 6:00 P.M. With spring in the air Herk, arriving first, sat at a table on the sidewalk. He had felt restless all day knowing what he planned, being cautious not to give any hint of his scheming posture to his colleagues, especially to Wolfe Hucksburgh.

As he waited for Arnold his mind was, at last, attracted away from his torment by the agreeable condition of the weather. It was warm, though not hot; there was a sort of glow to the twilight, and the sidewalk bustled with humans, all of whom seemed, at the moment, without pressing care. The ambiance had a curative effect on Herkimer. There was a freshness to the air, albeit a city kind of freshness, and he breathed deeply, expelling his sullen thoughts. He felt, now, as though he would, for certain, bring some honesty and justice to these unprincipled times in which he lived. The approach of Arnold, striding briskly, a smile inscribed on his face, gave further boost to Herk's spirits.

"Hey, Pal!" said Arnold taking a chair at the table.

"You look chipper," Herk observed.

"You bet. Couldn't be better."

"I was glad to hear you hadn't given up your apartment in these parts. I'm glad you moved back up here."

"I'm glad, too."

"And the energetic Ms. Rosen...?"

"Gone. Gone out of my life."

"Altogether?"

"Yep. She left the firm, a-n-nd, a-n-nd ... I inherited her job!"

"Terrific! And when did this happen?"

"Well, I moved out of her apartment a month ago. She went to work at Merrill, Lynch two weeks ago, and they told me of my new responsibilities just yesterday."

"Hey!" Herk gave Arnold a high five. "This is a celebration then. Waiter!" he called, signaling the young woman who bustled about amongst the tables. When she approached he said, "Bring us a bottle of Chablis."

"What, no Champaign?" Arnold chided.

"Can't stand it. The fizz hides the flavor and the bubbles go up my nose."

And so they settled in for a chat that would help to change Herkimer's life for so long as he had one.

"You sounded rather glum when you called today," said Arnold when they had settled down with the wine.

"I think serious would be more apt," said Herk. "And yes, I am. I am about to ask your help, once again, because of your familiarity with Washington and the bureaucracy. Oh, I don't intend to get you involved—beyond giving me an introduction to someone or other down there. I don't have any idea who."

He then explained to Arnold his concerns about the typhoid epidemic in Minneapolis and his, that is WWE's, possible connection.

"Wait a minute," Arnold said. "You think that possibly your guys got together with the bureaucrats in Minneapolis and didn't put in those machines at all?"

"I think it's quite possible that they all conspired to put in much cheaper machines and charged the industries full price for what they claim are cold fusion engines."

"H-m-m." Arnold pondered. "Then you think maybe the whole 'cold fusion' idea is a hoax?"

"I don't think so. I did enough study on this new technology to know it's quite possible. In fact, I almost took a job with an outfit who developed the cold fusion engine and is building them. In the course of deciding where I should work I made a study of this new technological breakthrough. I really believe it will work and can help us keep the planet safe for humans. Dammit! I took that Goddam job for the same feeble reason anyone else would take a job—for money. So I guess I'm as much a charlatan as any of them."

"Don't be so hard on yourself. You didn't know what these guys were up to."

"Greed! That's what rules this age we're in. Nothing but greed! And I got myself involved in it." Herk was once again feeling the anguish which had been with him all day.

"But you're going to do something about this one, right?" Arnold said.

"I need your help."

Arnold, who had easily read the change in his old friend's attitude from that of confidence to uncertainty, leaned forward and, in earnestness, said, "Listen, old buddy, if there is anything—anything I can do for you, I will."

"Did you know anyone in the Environmental Protection Agency in Washington?"

This caused Arnold to grin. "Yes. Certainly I did. You must remember I worked for the Petroleum Institute. We had plenty of contact with the EPA."

"Well, do you know anyone there I might contact—tell my doubts about this...this fraud which I suspect? Someone who might want to help me get to the bottom of it?"

"Well," Arnold said, with a mischievous look, "I do have a couple of markers that I might call in."

And so he did. Arnold re-established contact with his former associates at the Petroleum Institute, exercising extreme precaution that they would not detect the motive of his friend, Herk. He did, of course, reveal to them that it was Herkimer Hampton, not Arnold Schwarz, who was in need of some assistance.

The lobbyists then, after having made Herk's acquaintance, introduced him to a gentleman at EPA, one Richard "Rick" Snoups, who was to prove the ideal contact, given the nature of Herk's intent.

Before taking himself to Washington Herkimer had deemed it judicious to advise his superior, Hucksburgh, of his intent. He did so in the manner of proffering an idea that could, perhaps, create for WWE an advantage over the competition.

"Have we ever informed the EPA of the total efficiency of our cold fusion machine?" he asked of his boss one day.

"Of course not!" Hucksburgh seemed incensed by the very notion. "You think we want them giving it out to every two-bit disposal company?"

"But we have an exclusive, don't we?"

"Hah! I can see you don't know the way things work in Washington. You can't trust any of those bastards down there."

"Well, I was going to Washington this weekend to see a friend of mine. He knows some guys at the EPA."

"Listen," Hucksburgh said, almost stepping on Herk's toes as he stepped forward, hovering above the subordinate, his face lowered so that noses nearly touched. "If you even go near those scum at EPA you're outa here. Understand?"

"Okay," Herk said, for he <u>did</u> understand—with far greater assurance than he had before this short encounter. He had been right. There was some fraud involved here. What else could cause his proposition to nettle his boss so profoundly? His resolve was intensified. He made preparation to travel to the D.C. on Friday, telling Hucksburgh he would be absent on that day. Though it caused him some anxiety, he was forced to prevaricate—an act he thoroughly despised—in assuring his superior of the innocence of his visit. He met Mr. Snoups for luncheon and their dialogue extended into the late afternoon.

"So you think that the epidemic may have been caused by faulty machines, machines that are far less efficient than advertised?" Snoups was a fellow of about equal height to Herk but of considerably leaner frame. He had a narrow face which made his eye sockets appear larger than actual; they dominated his countenance so that when Herk was subject to Snoups' gaze he felt pierced by an acuity which discerned his every notion.

"That's certainly a possibility, wouldn't you think?" Herk said.

"We had not considered that possibility," Snoups admitted, "though we certainly have been aware that the outbreak could—probably was—caused by pollution in the river. Hm-m-m." He looked away, cogitating. "And why," he continued, looking once more at Herk, gravely, "have you decided to come to us with this?"

"Because," Herk said, with equal gravity, "I am troubled by what I've read and ... and ... well, ashamed to think that I may have some responsibility. You see, I made the initial contact with the authorities out there, and when I expressed my concern at what has happened I was instructed, by my boss, to keep my mouth shut."

Snoups nodded as though in sympathy.

"I thought about simply resigning," Herk continued with ardor, "but if I did that I'd always feel guilty."

"So you want to help get to the bottom of this?"

Herk nodded.

"Have you ever done any investigating?"

"You mean like detective work? No, I haven't."

"In business, though, you've had to look into a situation, to put facts together so that you could come to some conclusion. You've had that experience."

"I think," said Herk with some irony, "that is called living.

Snoups came to the conclusion that they could use Herk's assistance in discerning whether there had been some fraud in connection with the problem in Minneapolis but advised our friend that he should probably resign from the employ of WWE. If he were to stay in his current position his superiors might suspect the investigation and hasten to cover their tracks with greater resolve.

"Can you get along without that income for the next few months?" asked Snoups, adding, "We can't put you on our payroll. That could invite a longer legal battle. If it's possible we don't want them to know we are making any kind of investigation. We may even have to employ the FBI—much as I distrust that branch of the bureaucracy."

Herkimer informed him that he could subsist for some months without the income from WWE. And so it was that, two weeks after his initial meeting with Mr. Snoups, Herkimer resigned his position with the disposal giant. Before doing so, however, he discovered, through subterfuge, the names of the companies which were on record as party to the transaction for purchase of the aforementioned machines. He promptly delivered the information to his new colleague, Richard Snoups. It was of great interest to Herkimer, in passing over the documents, to note that one of the concerns to which the machine had been sold was none other than Minnesota Feed And Seed, the company founded by Deeana's great grandfather and now headed by her brother, Wayne, a fact which troubled him somewhat but then, he reckoned, the CEO probably had no knowledge of how the disposal system worked or how the decision as to the supplier of the system was arrived at. Wayne he knew as a forthright and honorable person whom Herk found it difficult to imagine could be involved in a fraud so scurrilous as he imagined this affair to be. Still, he thought it best he discuss the possibilities with his spouse.

"Maybe I've got this all wrong," he said to her on a quiet evening when Penelope was ensconced for the night in her bed. "I finally got the list of all the firms which were sold this supposedly miracle machine by WWE."

"And...?"

"Minnesota Feed And Seed is on the list."

She looked away as though concentrating on an invisible vista, stared for a moment in thought, answered, "I was afraid that might be the case," and continued to stare.

"Uh...well, I guess I'd better just back out of this damned operation; let the Feds handle it." His voice showed his distress.

"Oh no," she said turning her gaze directly onto him. "You continue right on with it. I'm sure Wayne is not to blame for this horror." Then after a moment's silence she added, "Though the shame will rub off on him." After another moment's silence she added with great conviction, "But he'll have to face the consequences. You <u>must</u> work to uncover the culprits in this!"

With this assurance from Deeana, Herk resigned his position at WWE next day. When asked by Hucksburgh his reason, he replied, simply, that he was weary of work and intended a holiday of several months.

He did remain idle for a couple of weeks and it proved a propitious time for him to do so. He received word from Iowa that the Judge was suffering precarious health; he'd had a mild heart attack and the doctor had advised him that a period of indolence would be his most helpful remedy. Being heedful, the Judge had submitted his resignation to the Governor and repaired to the old house in Clayton. Herkimer was beset with apprehension. The Judge was beyond the accepted age of retirement, and, so, Herk had been prepared for the prospect of the Judge's inactive years. He was not prepared for the problem of poor health. Herk determined that he would proceed to the Homeland.

Herk had been assured by the Judge that "this heart thing" was but a minor nuisance and that he intended to return in a few months' time to the Capital as advisor to the Governor. By the time Herk arrived in Clayton, however, the Judge had suffered a second seizure. When Herk entered the old house on the hill he found his father confined to the four poster in which, as Herk recalled painfully, he had watched his mother pass through to the Great Beyond.

"Dad," Herk said upon entering the room which now incarcerated the old Judge, "you told me your attack was very slight, that a cleaning of your artery had made you good as new."

"Well," the Judge smiled, "I had a second little flutter. Nothing to worry about."

The Judge had been an angular man with broad shoulders and spare face, a tight jaw and acute pupils. Now his jowls were loose and his gaze, while still perceptive, no longer exhibited the quickness to which Herk was accustomed.

"Dad! Why aren't you in the hospital in Des Moines where you belong?"

"Oh, Doc Molloy is taking good care of me. Nothing like a good country doctor. No sir. They're far better than those specialists at those health facilities. Doc Molloy really cares—we've been friends for fifty years. He'll get me through this okay."

This short visit with his son was to be one of the last pleasures the old Judge would experience. Before it came time for Herkimer to return to New York the Judge was seized by a massive stroke from which he was carried into the Hereafter. Before this final failure of his heart, however, he had confided in Herkimer the terms of his final will. Those possessions of paper capital which he held were willed to Penelope, to be held in trust until she had attained maturity, skipping a generation and, therefore, putting off the taxation. The old house in which he died was willed to the woman who had cared for it all those years, the same woman who had been Herk's guardian for that short period in his adolescence. The Home Place, the name they gave to the farm land and house which Herk's great grandfather had settled upon the cessation of hostilities in 1865, was willed to Herk with the provision that Herschel Wildt, the man who had farmed it and shared in the proceeds all the years the Judge had owned it, should remain as proprietor throughout his—Wildt's—lifetime.

While it was a somber time for Herkimer, he felt, nonetheless, fortunate that he was with the Judge in those last days and that he had been accorded this opportunity to establish an adult relationship with the old man which he had not before enjoyed. The old man spoke with him, reminiscing on his own earlier days, so that Herk was invested with a more comprehensive knowledge of his heritage than he had before enjoyed. Herk also thought it fortunate that he had not asked Deeana and Penelope to accompany him. It would have been a trial for the little girl and an unnecessary burden on his wife.

Upon the burial of the Judge, a service attended by a multitude of dignitaries from around the state, Herk stayed on a few days to supervise the execution of the terms of the Judge's will. This was accomplished with a minimum of effort. During the course of this Herkimer decided it advisable that he not only assure the Wildt's continuance on the Home Place by terms of the will, he set in motion the paper work which would deed the property to them and their heirs in perpetuity. This accomplished he felt comfortable in returning to New York to rejoin his family.

It was the last comfort he was to feel for some time, for he was immediately faced with the conundrum of what to do about his responsibilities to mankind and the Environmental Protection Agency.

XIV

When Herk returned from his painful journey Deeana informed him that he had received, on the answering machine, several messages from Rick Snoups urging him to return the calls. She handed him the D.C. phone number transcribed from the machine and he promptly dialed it. Snoups himself answered.

"Can you come down to Washington for a meeting—tomorrow?" Snoups asked. "We're getting some guys from the FBI involved and they'd like to hear from you what you've got to tell."

"Well..." this frightened even the intrepid Herkimer Hampton, but he didn't see how he could stop now. "I guess so."

"We'll buy your ticket on the shuttle."

The meeting was to occur at ten A.M. in Snoups' office so Herk was at Laguardia Airport at eight the following morning still fretting over the idea of being in the room with FBI agents. He had heard many tales of FBI duplicity, and he wondered if, in fact, they might not turn on him and try to insinuate his culpability so that they would not be required to go through the process of ferreting out the guilty individuals.

His fears were allayed when he met the two agents of the FBI, Wilfred Hunt, a skinny man with an overly large nose, and Ralph Quester, a squat fellow with large ears protruding prominently from his cranium. Both greeted Herk with a smiling heartiness and expressed the hope that, together, they might uncover some foul play and bring the bastards responsible to justice. They were soon joined by Snoups' assistant, Ms. Eva Avid, a quite attractive woman of thirty something with a shock of ebony hair curled about her slender face. She was dressed unlike any other of the Washington women Herk had seen. She wore slacks of khaki, a matching khaki colored blouse of silk or rayon and white sneakers for shoes. She approached Herk boldly, took his hand, and, looking him directly in the eye—for she was of equal height—pumped vigorously.

"So you're the brave guy who came forward with information," she said. "This country needs people like you. Too many sharks out there who only care about the buck."

Herk, at a loss, simply smiled and nodded.

Snoups, who had been sitting silent at his desk, suddenly became activated. He sprang from his chair and paced the floor. "Sit! Sit!" he commanded Herk and Ms. Avid, pointing to the only seating vacant, a love seat sized sofa against one wall. Eva promptly acceded, leaving one cushion open. Herk after carefully sizing the situation, seeing no other vacancy, with caution, placed himself beside the titillating assistant, being careful to move as far as possible to one side.

"Now," Snoups began, "we have made tests of the river water. We tested above the locale where all the factories begin; we tested just outside each factory, and we tested below the factories. It would appear that Mr. Hampton's fears are justified."

Snoups sat back in his chair and folded his hands across his belly, affecting an air of supreme satisfaction.

"Above the factories there is very little pollution, nothing that might infect one with a serious malady. Where the river flows alongside the factories the pollution is high and we have detected particles which, if ingested in even a minute amount, might cause a serious lowering of immunity in the system so that germs would find a receptive place for growth. We found these alien particles in the water for several miles down stream but none upstream from the factories. It appears that those plants are releasing harmful waste into the water—and quite probably the atmosphere—at greaser rates than in previous years."

They sat in silence for several seconds, considering the import of Snoups' message, until Hunt, who seemed the sharper of the two Federal agents, made an observation.

"Well," he said, "I think you've got 'em dead to rights. You won't be needin' us for this one."

"It's not quite so simple," said Snoups. "We're looking at fraud here—fraud on the part of some government officials and the people at WWE. Maybe some guys at the factories, too. We really need some proof on them. They should be punished."

There was another moment of silence and Hunt said, "What we need is a mole."

"A mole?" Except as the name of a small animal Herk was unfamiliar with the term.

"Someone to get into a place where we can get some of the records on the transactions for those machines, prove who contracted to buy 'em, who really did the sellin' and what was promised," Hunt answered.

"Of course," said Snoups. "We need to know the city officials involved <u>and</u> how much they got for selling them. If it's what I think there was considerable graft involved." He turned to Herk. "How much did you say those machines sold for?"

"I didn't say," Herk answered. "The price I was told to quote was a million five hundred thousand apiece. But I was never allowed to make the final deal. My boss, and the President always did that."

After some discussion it was decided that perhaps the best way to get the information they wanted was to secure a position for their mole in the finance department of one of the companies in Minneapolis. There, they would probably have access to files where they might find evidence as to just what individuals were involved in the contracting of the purchase—who from both sides, seller and purchaser. They could learn the purchase price, too. They decided they needed this covert operation so that those involved would not become aware of their investigation and attempt to cover their tracks.

Snoups first asked Herk if he would take on this assignment as it was known that he qualified as a CPA, but Herk objected.

"My brother-in-law runs one of the factories. If he found I was working in any of those plants—and I don't think we could keep it from him—he'd want to know why."

"Well, Ms. Avid," said Snoups, "it seems the assignment must fall to you. You are a qualified accountant, I believe."

Eva admitted to her mastery of this discipline and, while not excited at the prospect of being a mole, reluctantly agreed to accept the assignment.

It was advanced by Hunt that perhaps she should have some stalwart support if something unforeseen occurred, and so it was decided that Herk should also be sent, undercover, as a sort of guardian to Ms. Avid.

When Herk informed Deeana that he must absent himself for some time, to find employment in Minneapolis, while a bit unnerved, she replied that she would go too, that she and Penelope could stay with her parents.

"I don't think that would be a good idea," Herk hastened to inform her. "It will be very important that no one connected in any way to any of these companies know that I even exist. Your brother should never suspect that I am in Minnesota."

Deeana, while a bit disturbed to know she should be alone with her daughter for some time, nonetheless, understood the advisability of this precaution. She accepted with equanimity.

With some help from Hunt and Quester he affected his arrival in Minneapolis in a seven year old Ford Escort which looked as though it might have been retrieved from a junk yard. The two Federal agents accompanied him to Chicago where they purchased the auto. While the engine, transmission and suspension were restored to the state of a much newer vehicle, the body and interior were left as found, shabby to the eye. Herk then drove from Chicago to Minneapolis.

During the time it took to perform these tasks Ms. Avid had been transported to Minneapolis. Through some clandestine string-pulling by the Feds she had acquired employment as an associate in the finance department, where all records were stored, at Hennepin Paper, one of the companies which had purchased the WWE disposal system. Herk was given a telephone number where he could reach her.

Ms. Avid had acquired a small, furnished apartment, and Herk was instructed that he should call her only there and never to leave a message on an answering machine, neither there nor anywhere else in the Twin Cities. He was to find housing in some cheap apartment in a seedy section of the city, down along the river front, and not far distant from the manufacturing section where the plants under suspicion were all located. He was then to apply for employment as a clean-up man, or, preferably, night watchman at the Hennepin Paper factory. The Feds had supplied him with a certificate which attested that he had successfully completed a course which made him proficient in security work so that he might present it to the superintendent at Hennepin when making application. Hunt and Quester then effected the removal of the current night-watchman at the plant by securing for him a more remunerative position at a packing plant in Austin, a town far enough from Minneapolis to assure that he was out of the way yet close enough to allay suspicion.

And so Herkimer was ensconced in a one room lodging and employed by those he had come to investigate, but only after a rather strange interview with the plant superintendent. William "Bull" O'Dour was a broad man of about six feet in height, a face of angular jowls festooned with bristly whiskers. One could see immediately whence came his sobriquet. He looked as though he might leap into a pit for a bit of a grapple at a moment's prodding. He also carried with him a considerable brogue.

"Now tell me, son, what brings y' ta Minneapolis? What's wrong 'uth Chicago?"

"I have always liked Minneapolis," was the most sane answer which came quickly to Herk's mind.

"I see. And y' seem ta be fairly ed-ee-cated." O'Dour's smile was not so much a show of good nature as of irony.

"Well, Sir, no more than others I grew up with."

"Sir, is it? We have a prig on our hands, do we?" O'Dour smiled sarcastically at Herk.

"No Sir," Herk said with as little inflection as possible.

"I don't suppose y' could be runnin' from somethin', could y'?" This time the Bull's gaze was severe.

Herk was intimidated, at a loss for direct reply. "I...I...don't understand."

"Y' don't, eh!" The Bull moved in close to Herk and arched one brow. "Drugs?"

Now Herk was indignant.

"No, Sir!" he said with a firm finality an unbiased observer would take as absolute assurance.

"No, eh?" The Bull persisted.

"Sir!" Herkimer said with increasing fervor. "I have never touched an illegal drug. I have not associated with people who do!"

O'Dour stepped back now, apparently satisfied. "Just want y' ta know," he said without irony, "that I don't tolerate the use—even off the job."

"I appreciate that, Sir," said Herk, and he almost felt as though he should fling the Bull a salute.

From this moment their relationship progressed to one of mutual respect. O'Dour was not nearly so sever as he had given Herk to believe in their first interview. In fact, Bull O'Dour seemed happy to see Herk when they met each day. Herk's shift was a long one—from ten in the evening until eight o'clock the following morning when he would be relieved by the day time janitor and O'Dour who worked a ten hour day, not unusual in this era of downsizing workers and upsizing profits.

"Another uneventful night was it, me Lad?" the Bull would ask.

"Nothing happened so far as I know," Herk would reply.

"Well, a good lad such as you would surely know how ta fix it if anythin' went wrong."

So, having gained the confidence of the plant superintendent, Herk considered his first important task a success. It was thus that he became confident enough in his relations with O'Dour that he raised the question of the epidemic of diseases and the media speculation, which had not abated, as to the possible culpability of the manufacturers.

"No way," said O'Dour. "Why we got the best waste disposal equipment there is. Brand new just a year ago. Sure an' the media got nuthin' better t' do with their damned time."

"The newest and best," said Herkimer, affecting false wonder, a thing he was not accustomed to do. "Gee! Where is it?"

"I'll show it t' y'." said the scrappy Irishman. And he promptly led Herk to a room at the end of the factory and pointed toward a large and very complex looking machine, nothing like the simple looking machines Herk had been shown at Tomorrow Incorporated. He made a decision to phone the fellow with whom he had been friendly at those cold fusion developers.

That very morning he made the call. Arming himself with a pocketful of coins he found a pay phone, ensconced in a glass booth, along a thoroughfare near his humble habitat. The fellow's name, Herk remembered quite readily, was George Bonhomme, clearly of French extraction, and, by seeking aid from the telephone information service, he discovered the number of Tomorrow Incorporated and dialed it.

Upon receiving an answer from the female voice, which professed to be Tomorrow Incorporated, he asked for Mr. George Bonhomme. The pulse was immediately switched to where a second female voice proclaimed, "Mr. Bonhomme's office."

"May I speak with him, please?" said Herk.

"Who may I say is calling?"

"Herkimer Hampton. He knows me from a couple of years ago when I was looking for a job."

The voice disappeared, and, in a moment, a male voice gave a robust greeting as though pleased to have been summoned.

"Hell-o-oh! Is this Herkimer Hampton, indeed?"

"Yes, it is. Hello, Mr. Bonhomme."

"Don't tell me. You've decided you want to work for us after all."

"Well, that's not why I called but it might not be a bad idea. What I called about, I really just wanted some information if you wouldn't mind. Something that could help me in what I'm doing right now."

"Shoot," came Bonhomme's reply. "If I can be of any help I will."

"Well, could you tell me how many of your cold fusion machines were purchased by my former employers World Without End?"

"Former employers? Then you could come to work for us," Bonhomme chirruped. "But that's not what you asked, is it? Well, Herkimer, we haven't sold any cold fusion machines to anyone. There were a few too many glitches. We're still working on it. I don't know if we'll ever get that one right. Give us another year or two. If we can't get it we'll give up. We already have the best disposal systems in the business so we aren't worried."

"You've sold none?" Herkimer said with a note of finality, for he had surely discovered what he needed. "None at all?" he repeated.

"That's right," said Bonhomme. "Why are you asking?"

"Oh, some guy told me about this machine his company has which is supposed to work by cold fusion. I didn't think any other company but yours had it."

"They don't. And neither do we. We do hold a patent so that when—if—it's ever perfected it will be by us. As I say, though, we have, already, the best systems in the business, so if you want to work for us come on over and talk."

This was pleasing for Herk to hear. It gave him a felicitous feeling he had not enjoyed in some time.

"I just may do that," he said. "And thank you. One more thing. Did you sell any machines at all to World Without End?"

"Nope," came the reply. "We don't do business with them. We don't trust their CEO. I'm glad you're not working for them any longer."

This made Herk feel better. He was pleased to hear this concord on the perfidy of the clearly evil Dewar. He was also relieved to know that the good people at Tomorrow Inc. could not be implicated in the scam.

Herk reported this additional verification of his original suspicion to Rick Snoups in Washington.

"Good," said Snoups after Herk had given him this latest information. "We've got enough to close down those factories, but we still need to know just who was involved in the sale of those machines. Eva is working on that but hasn't reported in yet. I think she's afraid they might catch onto what she's up to. Maybe you should give her a little prod."

Herk, although it had been against his orders, immediately called Hennepin headquarters and asked for Ms. Avid.

"Who shall I say is calling?" came a whiny voice.

Herkimer had to think fast. "Just a friend from back East," he said. "Make her guess," he added in a jocular tone.

"I'll try," the voice whined.

"Yes?" came the curt voice of Eva Avid after a short wait.

"It's me, Herkimer."

"Oh, Mr. Harris," came the formal reply. "If you'll meet me after work I'll give you the application. I'll buy dinner at—let's say—**The Haufbrau House** at six o'clock. Okay?"

"That's fine," Herk answered and the line went dead. Eva was, obviously, a bit surprised he had called her there.

And so, after a four hour nap in his sleazy chambers, Herk repaired to **The Haufbrau House** in mid-town Minneapolis, dressed, for the first time in this sojourn, as a reputable business type, in suit and tie. Eva appeared in more formal attire than Herk had, prior to this, been aware was part of her wardrobe. Her ebony hair was pulled back close along her temples and secured in back by a silver brooch; her black dress, so snug it seemed of elastic, ended above her knees and was offset by a loose red smock of translucent material so light it wafted behind her as she moved toward him, splendid bosoms pointing the way. A rather large leather handbag was slung on a long strap from one shoulder, and in the opposite hand she carried a portfolio containing papers which she tossed onto the table at which Herk had placed himself to await this moment.

"Hi, stranger," she ejaculated pleasantly.

"Hello, Eva," Herk replied. "I've wanted to call you but was afraid of being discovered."

As Eva took her seat she said, "I don't think we need to worry anymore. I think we've got the evidence we need right here." And she pointed to the portfolio of papers.

Being eager to learn the depths of her enquiry, Herk opened the portfolio and laid the papers on the table even before they inspected the restaurant menu.

"There," said Ms. Avid, looking across the angle of the table and pointing to a line at the bottom of a page. "I believe you can decipher the signature as that of Dean Wilkie."

Indeed he could. While the penmanship would scarcely pass a grade school exercise it was recognizable as Dean Wilkie, City Treasurer.

Herk nodded. "So they bought the machines directly from the City—or, I should say—from Wilkie." And after studying the paper a moment more he looked up and said, "You know. I looked at the machine in the Hennipen plant. It's nothing like the cold fusion machine I saw at Tomorrow Incorporated. Besides, this guy at Tomorrow told me they haven't sold a machine yet. They haven't even perfected it."

"So let's have a little celebration," said Ms. Avid. "This calls for champagne."

"Uh...no..." said Herk. "How about some Cabernet Sauvignon? I don't like champagne."

"Whatever you say," she replied. "You're the hero in this drama."

They quaffed a magnitude of wine and dined on roast prime ribs of beef. The serving was so large that even Herk, known for a prodigious appetite, left a sizeable chunk on his plate.

Herk kept with him the incriminating documents as they left the restaurant. They were both a bit in the grasps of Master Barleycorn and wavered slightly as they strode out onto the sidewalk. As they were about to separate, Eva took Herk by the arm and insinuated her pliable bosom to his biceps.

"Aren't you going to see me home?" she asked in a teasing tone.

"Sure," said Herk and hailed a taxi.

Ensconced in the cab Ms. Avid slipped her frame toward Herk's side until her thigh was firm against his and once again seized his arm in both her hands. This made him quite uncomfortable. He had been fearful of Ms. Avid—one of the reasons he had not contacted her previously. Perhaps we should say he was fearful of his own propensity to lust, for it required some resolve for him to decline her invitation to come inside and survey her quarters when they arrived outside her building.

"No," he said. "I have to go to work at ten o'clock. First I have to go home and change."

"Just for a few minutes," she said. "It's only eight-fifteen. Besides, very shortly you'll be through with that job. We've got all we need on them and it's time to blow the whistle. So come on in."

"'Fraid not," Herk said. "I want to make some phone calls. I'll talk to you tomorrow." And he closed the door of the cab and quoted, for the driver, the street and number of his grubby abode. Then, extracting his handkerchief, he wiped the perspiration from his brow.

After his night of labor, during which he could scarcely recline on the chair provided him due to his state of agitation at both his near miss with Ms. Avid and anticipation of the action he imagined for the following day, he collected the coins he had saved for the telephone and made his way to the familiar booth.

He dialed Washington D.C. and Rick Snoups. "I think we've got all we need," he said and told Snoups about the documents with Wilkie's name on them.

"Okay," said Snoups, "we'll move on this."

And move they did—at both ends. In New York, Quester secured a search order and examined the files of WWE. In Minneapolis, Hunt accomplished the same with all four manufacturers as well as the City Finance Department. The revelations were nothing short of astounding. WWE bought the machines in question from a company in Texas which had built them in Mexico. WWE paid 250,000 dollars apiece for them and sold them, according to their books, for 500,000 each to the City of Minneapolis. According to the City Treasurer's account the machines had been purchased for 650,000 dollars each and sold to the manufacturers for 750,000 per machine. From the accounts of the four companies they appeared to have paid a million each for the non-functional engines. Since all papers had been signed on behalf of all three entities concerned, it appeared that a giant fraud, which involved individuals from each, had been committed, for the numbers on the different receipts had wide variation. When confronted with this fact the managers of the plants, as though in accord, pointed to the City Treasurer, Dean Wilkie, as he who had recommended— perhaps insisted would be more accurate—that they install the disposal systems in question.

It seems that one of these managers, or perhaps someone of lesser stature but greater propensity for gossip, had broadcast the events of the search. By the time Wilfred Hunt, accompanied by Herkimer, who knew the miscreant on sight, had assaulted the vaults of City Hall, Mr. Wilkie had disappeared. Herkimer, however, spotted and identified Wilkie's three associates, Hefty and the two smaller ones, who were promptly asked to accompany the FBI agents to the Federal offices for questioning.

Herk was included in this inquiry and, indeed, he felt almost as though he were under suspicion during the interrogation. He saw after a moment, though, that the government agents treated him thus as a subterfuge.

The three bureaucrats sat alongside one wall. Herk sat at an angle to them along another, all four faced, across a broad desk, to Snoups and Hunt.

"Now," began Snoups the inquisitor, "we have brought you here to help us find the truth about some waste disposal systems which we believe are quite defective and could be the cause of the epidemic sickness suffered in one particular area of the city."

Snoups looked to them for some reaction but got nothing save silent stares as he made a quick grin and directed his gaze to Herk.

"You, Hampton," said Snoups as though addressing a stranger, "you are purported to have sold the machines in question to these gentlemen."

"No, Sir," Herk said, feeling still quite uneasy. "I made contact with them for my company, WWE, but I didn't make any sale. They insisted on speaking with my CEO."

"Right. Of course. But nonetheless they prevailed upon the companies to buy these machines. And by they I believe I am speaking of these three, am I not?" he was still directing his questions to Herk.

"Well, no Sir," Herk answered. "It wasn't actually any of them, I don't believe. I believe it was the City Treasurer, Mr. Dean Wilkie."

"And he is not here?"

"No, Sir."

Snoups directed his eyes at Hefty. "And where *is* this Mr. Wilkie, pray tell?" There was silence.

"You!" Snoups pointed to Hefty. "I'm asking you directly. I expect an answer."

Hefty made a move sideways in his chair as though to put more distance between himself and his two accomplices. He grunted and then forced a muffled answer, "I don't know."

"You don't know." Snoups spoke with disdain, then turned to Hunt. "Well, Wilfred, looks like we may have a good case for obstruction of justice here. What kind of sentence does that carry?"

Hunt looked at the three under suspicion, a wry grin across his features. "One to ten I reckon," he said, obviously pleased to bring forth these numbers.

One of the nondescripts shifted in his chair. For the first time Herkimer noticed some vital signs in his face. His eyes projected fear, terror.

"Listen," he said in a whiney voice, "I ain't going to jail for that damned Wilkie, but I don't know where he went. He just disappeared. He can't be found at his home. He's a bachelor and I don't have any idea how to trace him. If I did I'd tell you."

Snoups and Hunt looked at each other, and Snoups nodded as though to indicate Hunt should proceed with his probe.

"Well now, isn't that interesting! Wilkie scrammed and left you guys to take the blame." Hunt turned his head and pointed to Herkimer. "This fellow can testify that you three were present when he sold Wilkie on the idea of requiring standards that would necessitate one of those cold fusion machines in all factories within the City Limits. He's already agreed to take a dive for his company's part in this scam."

All three miscreants stared at Herk. In the eyes of Hefty Herk read malevolence; in those of the other two he saw only fear.

"Mr. Hampton," Hunt continued, "do you recognize these characters?"

"Yes, Sir," Herk answered.

"Tell us how."

"I came out here as a representative of WWE to try to sell some cold fusion machines. My boss thought I should start with city officials to see what their reaction would be to a machine that totally eliminated the dangers from refuse."

"And these three met with you?" Hunt continued.

"These three and Mr.Wilkie, the City Treasurer."

"And what did you discuss?"

"Well, I showed them all about this new kind of machine. I had a video which explains the whole thing."

"And what was the reaction?"

"At the time there was no reaction, but when I got back to New York Mr. Wilkie phoned and asked if I would set up a meeting for them with my president."

"And did you?"

"Yes."

"What happened?"

"Well, I was never brought into the negotiations, but I know that, shortly after, WWE sold several machines in Minneapolis."

"Do you know anything about this?" Hunt directed his question at the three bureaucrats, but they sat silent.

"How about you, Mr. Wimple?" Hunt directed this at one of the two nondescripts, and he immediately moved forward in his chair and cast his eyes toward Herkimer.

"This guy sold us a bill of goods," Wimple shouted, pointing a finger at Herk. And for the first time Herk saw evidence of intelligence in his expression of anger.

"How's that?" Hunt asked sarcastically.

"He told us he had these machines that would make the waste totally—totally clean. Then he told us we ought to get our City Council to make it illegal to permit anything less."

"And did you try this?" Hunt was enjoying himself.

"You bet we did. And now you're telling us we're responsible for toxic waste. We did everything they told us to do."

"You got the companies along the river to install these machines?" Hunt continued.

"Wilkie did I guess."

"And they bought them through you—not directly from WWE?" Hunt was becoming more aggressive.

"I don't know. We never got involved beyond that first meeting—with this guy." He pointed to Herk.

"We know," Hunt said, actually grinning, "that the sale passed through your hands." Hunt picked up some papers, which were before him, as though to inspect them. "We have the documents right here which show that you bought them for five hundred thousand each..." He ruffled through some other papers he had before him. "And then," he continued, "you sold them for a million and a half each. Times four and you'll get a profit, of perhaps, four million—for someone." He looked directly at Wimple. "Where did all that profit go? To the City?"

"Well," said Wimple, quite flustered. "I guess it did."

"You guess?" Hunt was really boring in now.

"Mr. Wimple," he continued, "I suggest that a lot of that money went into your pockets—the three of you and Wilkie, and perhaps some people at the plants. You profited richly from these sales, didn't you?"

Hunt was silent, awaiting an answer but none came. The three sat impassive until, after several moments, Hefty spoke.

"I want a lawyer," he said.

"You'll have one," Hunt continued. "You sold them to the companies involved for one million and a half each—probably half a million dollars profit from each machine. You're all entitled to legal defense."

The litigation took six months. The only crime committed was that of fraud. They couldn't be charged for all the sickness caused. Dewar and Hucksburgh claimed that the people who sold the machines to them had promised the level of clean which they, in turn, had promised to the people of Minneapolis. The people from the company in Texas were never uncovered. Their outfit had gone out of business.

Dewar and Hucksburgh were fined a million dollars each and forbidden to work in the disposal field ever again. The three plant managers, since they were implicated in Wilkie's swindle, were convicted of fraud but got off with fines of one hundred thousand dollars each and suspended sentences. The three city officials were also given suspended sentences with no fines since it was established that each got no more for their silence than a few hundred dollars from Wilkie, the true culprit. Wilkie, of course, would have been heavily fined, and even perhaps, incarcerated, but he was never discovered.

So in all, nine heads rolled, for none of those involved would again be employed by their respective institutions. WWE, of course, went out of business. The current whereabouts of Dewar and Hucksburgh, like that of Wilkie, is unknown. The plant managers left Minneapolis for more cordial environs, as did the three City Hall bureaucrats.

Thus ended one of Herkimer's most painful labors, one which left him unemployed and unsure of his future.

XV

The cold fusion scam received considerable coverage by journalists, not only in Minneapolis but throughout the United States. One might suppose that a bit of celebrity would aid Herk in a search for re-employment; it did not. The press, in its voracity for calumny, had dredged up Wolfe Hucksburgh who appeared on nationwide TV. Hucksburgh attempted, verbally, to challenge Herk's credibility; they had never promised what Herk claimed they had. He, Herkimer Hampton, had fabricated the efficacy of those machines so that he, Herkimer, might benefit from the sale.

Of course, the EPA and FBI knew that this was not the case. Wimple, the Minneapolis bureaucrat had, under examination, verified Herk's story. He had been present when the sale was contracted by his boss, Wilkie, with Hucksburgh and Dewar. These facts were attested by Hunt in an Evening News interview but most of the journalists preferred to highlight the claims of the supervisor, Hucksburgh, because Herkimer refused their offer of celebrity and chose not to go on the tube in his own defense. Thus Herk found himself defamed in the minds of most of those who might have offered him employment.

Herkimer was hardly distraught, however. There was sustenance enough in the larder to allow him, Deeana and Penelope to maintain a quite decent mode of life. As we have seen, in his remunerative periods of labor he had accumulated considerable funds against just such a situation as he now experienced. There was also the estate of the Judge which had been willed in trust to Penelope. Some funds from that might be employed for her education should the need arise.

Still, the uncertainty of the small family's future was perturbing. Herk and Deeana were now beyond the age of thirty; little Penelope was almost five, approaching her entrance into school. As middle age beckoned Herk did not look with fervor on the pointless existence of total leisure, nor did Deeana. They decided that, with summer upon them, they would purchase their first automobile—they had never felt the need of one while living in Manhattan—and journey out into the vast expanses of these United States. Principally, they would spend some weeks in visiting Deeana's family and Herk's homeland of Iowa. Herkimer, of course, did not relish the idea of a return to Minneapolis. His memories of his recent stay in that proud burgh were not exactly felicitous.

So it was they availed themselves of a lustrous mini-van and heeded Horace Greeley's call to the young to head West. Before they left, however, Herkimer, being the ever practical planner, stowed in the rear of the van a two gallon size can of gasoline against the possibility that they should ever find themselves in a long, barren stretch with a fuel tank at empty.

They began their journey on Interstate 80 passing through the Poconos, then the Appalachians, on across Pennsylvania to the plains of Ohio along the shore of Lake Erie. They paused for their first night in a small motel south of Cleveland, then pressed on across the flatlands of Indiana to their second sojourn in a motel just west of Chicago.

Penelope was quite adaptable to wayfaring. They chose motor courts with pools so that, each evening, the small girl and her parents dipped themselves into the soothing waters as ablution against the rigors of travel. Penelope would gambol in the children's pool and, after a night of resuscitation, mount the mini-van in high spirits for another day's journey.

They proceeded some miles north of Chicago, then forsook the interstate highway system to travel the more aesthetic landscape of back-roads Wisconsin. They were approaching their first terminus, Minneapolis. They drove through green forests interspersed with the blue of undefiled lakes. They spent one more night in a motor lodge, in a small town, and this time, instead of dunking themselves in cool agua—there was no pool—they restored their spirits sitting on a deck gazing across the woodlands to an expanse of shimmering water.

"This is better than the city," Herk said, looking to the far hills outlined brightly in the luminosity of the descending sun. "Why don't we stay out here?"

"Sounds good," said his congenial spouse. "But what would you do?"

"Well, I couldn't be a farmer." Herk smiled at the idea. "I always felt an aversion to farming. Early in my life I decided I would rather earn a living with my mind than with my hands."

"You've done well at it, my Dear. We don't really have to worry, do we?" It was a statement rather than a question.

"I could go back to school and become a lawyer. Or am I too old for that?"

"Sweetheart, you're only thirty-five. That's still young. At least I _feel_ young." She grinned.

"What's a lawyer, Papa?" asked little Penelope.

"A lawyer...?" Herk considered his answer carefully. "A lawyer is someone trained to help us make sure that justice is done in our society."

"Or injustice." Deeana smirked.

Herk looked into her face with a frown. "My father was a lawyer," he said to Penelope, speaking as though injured. "Your grandfather. He was also a judge which is a lawyer who has been appointed to tell the difference between what's right and what's wrong."

"Come on," Deeana said. "It was a joke—a kind of joke. Now-a-days most lawyers don't give a hoot about justice and you know it. All they care about is becoming famous and making a lot of money. Just like most everyone in our sick society."

"Me included, I suppose." Herk played the hurt little boy.

"No, my Darling. Not you. Why do you suppose I love you so. Didn't I see you leave a big money job for one you thought would give you a chance to do good for society?" She reached out and took his hand in hers and added with tenderness, "Only to see that turn sour."

He sighed sorrowfully and nodded.

"I'm sorry," she said, "but I don't think I'd like it if you were a lawyer. Your father came of age in another generation, one not so crass and full of greed."

They sat staring out across the landscape until Penny broke the silence.

"Papa, why are you so sad?"

The two adults looked at each other in realization of the tenor of their conversation. They both looked down at the little girl sitting before them on the deck.

"I'm not sad, Darling," Herk said. "I'm very happy. I have you and your mama." And he reached forward and drew the child into his lap, pressing her to his bosom. "I love you both very much and that's happiness."

Later, when Penelope was snuggled onto the folding cot and they lay side by side in the large bed, Deeana's head on his shoulder, Herk said very quietly, "I think I'll go back to school and become a teacher."

"All right!" she said, as a cheer more than mere acquiescence, and repeated it. "A-a-all right!"

Next day they drove back south to cross The Father of Waters and approach Minneapolis from below. They arrived at Deeana's patriarchal home on Lake Minnetonka mid-afternoon. The lake was west of the limits of the City about fifteen miles, close enough to be classified a suburb. It was a large body of water with innumerable coves and bays along which wound a narrow roadway. Herkimer followed this several miles further along the northern shore of the lake to arrive at the Wallis residence.

They were warmly received by Deeana's parents. Herk had been apprehensive. He was well known in the Twin Cities as the fellow who had blown the whistle on their corrupt officials in the disposal fiasco. He had, of course, brought some censure to the plants of manufacture, one of which was owned by the elder Mr. Wallis. The old gentleman proved, however, to be just that: a man of honorable sensibilities. He greeted Herk with hand on shoulder and a hearty handshake, and later he openly professed his approbation for what his son-in-law had done.

The Wallis estate—for it was far more than a simple dwelling—lay on a neck of land which projected into the waters of the lake and was entered through two pillars constructed of brick masonry. The house, though hardly what one would describe as a mansion, was, nonetheless, expansive. Also of brick construct it stood at the end of a circular drive and, from the rear, the purview was across a broad verandah to the lake. At the bottom of a broad sward, which descended to the shore, was a boat dock and, tied to this, a handsome launch.

During the two weeks they passed at the Wallis manor Penelope enjoyed the freedom to cavort on the greensward. Her grandparents nurtured a hound, a rather bulky Norwegian pooch who responded to the name Knute, and he accompanied her on romps down to the lakeside and into the thicket surrounding the lawn. On occasion all three members of the Hampton family would embark in the launch for a tour of the coves along the shores of Lake Minnetonka. These were interludes in which Herkimer felt himself most serene. The openness of the water, his distance from all humans save those he treasured, effected a kind of tranquility to which he was not accustomed.

In fact, he did not feel totally at ease in the situation at the Wallis home. They and their coterie of associates were of a class to whom sociality is a conformity, a charade. Deeana, having been absent from it many years, felt the vacuity of it as did Herk.

"I had forgotten how phony these people can be," she said to Herk one evening, returning from a dinner party to which her mother had coerced their attendance. "The same people talking the same drivel, week after week. I'd forgotten how boring life can be out here amongst the clans." She giggled. "It's like an Edith Wharton novel. Most of those people are inter-married—some even cousin-to-cousin. Thank you, my Darling, for keeping me away from this."

"I can't wait till you see how it is in my home town," he said. "At least, as I recall, the people are a bit more interesting. They have some genuine concerns, such as how to survive." And they both laughed at this.

Before they could take leave of the Twin Cities area, Deeana made known her need to replenish her supply of herbal panaceas. She was running low on ginseng, ginkoba and St. John's Wort and had doubts that she would find them so readily in Herk's small hometown as they would in this metropolis. One of her cousins had recommended a natural food store near the University in St. Paul, and she presumed upon Herk to transport her across the mighty Mississippi once again to that locale. With the directions she had received they found the merchant described and, upon stowing their vehicle in a parking lot, proceeded to the shop.

Upon entering Herk found the wares on exhibit of some interest and so, while Deeana proceeded to the counter where the herbs were displayed, he made investigation of the rows of shelves housing the countless exotic fruits and vegetables.

At the counter Deeana was approached by a short man of slender torso who moved with a slight limp, almost a hop. He wore large spectacles framed in black plastic and his lower face was veiled in a thick crop of whiskers though his head was bereft of filament. His eyes were lifted slightly at the corners giving him an Oriental aspect.

"May I help you, Madame?" he asked with servility, tucking his head in a quick bow.

"I would like some ginkoba, some ginseng and some St. John's Wort—enough to last perhaps three months."

Deeana cast a gaze about the shop, impressed by the volume of merchandise. She had not realized that there were quite this many varieties of natural foods. Her eyes paused for a moment on her spouse who was inspecting a package which he held in his hand and smiled.

"Your husband, is he?" came a voice from behind her and she turned again toward the bearded merchant, holding now, with both hands, several boxes.

"Yes." Deeana smiled at him.

"Aha," said he, "then I have a little gift for you. It comes with a purchase as large as yours." He took from the low pocket of his loose cardigan a small phial and placed it in Deeana's hand with a firm grip that drew her fingers tightly around the small glass container. Bowing low, close to her face, he continued in a hushed voice, "If his interest in you should ever lag; if he should profess weariness or depression as reason for not performing his spousal duties, a half of this mixed into his wine or coffee will cause a wondrous transformation in his passions." Through the thick lenses of his spectacles, his slightly slanted eyes took on a glow which, had she not been more interested in the object he had bestowed, Deeana might have seen as evil.

For evil it was. Behind the dense disguise of beard and surgically slanted eyes lurked the dark soul of Mr. Dean Wilkie, the man whom Herkimer's persistence in the cold fusion affair had caused to forego his previous life and secrete himself as an Oriental tradesman. He had recognized Herk from their one meeting, his memory freshened by the photos which had appeared in newspapers upon the revelation of the fraud. Wilkie was, of course, raging behind his mask. What was in the phial presented, Deeana did not have a clue, but she surmised that it might relieve her husband in his, now frequent, moments of depression.

Deeana stowed the small bottle in the shopping bag with her restoratives and forgot about it. A day later they had their little van loaded and were on the road to Southern Iowa. As they passed the border into Herkimer's home state they began to drive through fields, to both right and left, where row upon row of corn stretched in perfectly parallel design as far as the horizon. It was early August and the green stalks had reached above the height of surrounding fences.

They took repast at a fast food depot outside Des Moines and, by four P.M., they found themselves approaching Clayton. Since Herk's childhood home had been given over, on the Judge's demise, to the woman who had maintained it all those years the Judge was away at the Capital, it was necessary that they take lodging at the one motel of the town. It was located alongside the highway on which they approached. The rooms were very small and there was no folding cot available for Penelope, so they found it necessary to engage two rooms, one with a pair of twin beds where Deeana would take repose with the child. Herk must slumber alone in a chamber adjacent.

After replenishing their appetites in the diner near the motel, they slept well the first night through. The following day they went to the house where Herk had grown to adolescence and called upon Ms. Hepzibah North, the lady who had exercised the position of caretaker through the years for the Judge and was now mistress of the manor.

Heppy, as acquaintances addressed her, was a lady somewhat beyond her fortieth year. She was of medium height for a woman, which is to say she was approximately that of Herk. She was of dark mien, slim but full of bosom, dressed in a loose, one piece dress which flared below her knees and was clasped snugly around the neck. Heppy was, indeed, the same robust woman who had, those many years previous, initiated Herk into the mysteries of carnality. The same languid, green eyes, into which he had gazed with propinquity those twenty odd years before, inspired in him the same trust they had at that time.

"Hi Heppy," he said with a smile.

"Banty!" she cried, delighted, and sprang to seize him about the neck.

Herk was a bit embarrassed at the ardor of her greeting—old guilts never seem to leave us—and stepped back, turning to Deeana who stood, holding Penelope by the hand, looking on from the edge of the porch across which he had approached the door.

"This is my wife and daughter," Herk said, grinning bravely though he felt queasy as he noticed Deeana's disapproving eye cast on Hepzibah.

"Oh," said Heppy, and still ebullient she stepped forward and extended her hand. "Hello. Pleased to meet you."

Deeana took her hand and forced a smile while Penelope nodded, her head down, and held more tightly to her mother's hand.

Ms. North invited them in to inspect the family home. It was much as Herk remembered it; even the furnishings were those of his mother.

"Do you live here alone?" Deeana asked as they tramped through the dining room occupied by a long hardwood table, eight chairs and a handsome cabinet, shelves lined with attractive blue and white ornamental China plates, cups and saucers, interspersed with delicate figurines, all former possessions of the late mistress of the household, Mrs. Hampton.

"Yes," said their hostess. "I never felt it necessary to marry. And besides," she cast the words over her shoulder as she lead them up the stairs, "after Banty left our town there was no one to measure up."

This enraged Deeana, but she maintained her serenity until they had completed their inspection of the premises and were in the van proceeding on their familiarization tour of the town.

"That's her, isn't it?" she said as they traveled, the two of them forward and Penny in the rear.

"What do you mean?" Herk affected innocence.

"You know what I mean. That's the woman who ..." she sought the proper term that Penny might be spared knowledge, "who introduced you to ... to life's pleasures!"

Herkimer was silent. Before they had married, in a spirit of total honesty, he had admitted to Deeana the sexual experience of his adolescence. He had assured her that, not since that time, had he defiled woman with his seed. She had accepted his confession, forgiven him, and professed her own virginity. Neither had since alluded to the subject.

Hekimer, however, had seemed, of late, to be somewhat distant and disinterested. He was, in truth, depressed. His adventure into the realm of ecology, which had ended so disastrously, had prompted, in him, a spirit of denial. Life—no people, not life—he had decided were more evil than good. He was suffering a spiritual depression. Deeana, feeling a loss of his usually cheery support, attributed it to disinterest in her. And now he had been reunited with this seductress. Deeana knew that it was probably absurd to attribute anything to this meeting, but, with Herk's current disposition, thoughts even of abandonment came into her consciousness.

"And what's this 'Banty' stuff?" she asked. "Is that your lovey-dovey name?"

"Everyone out here calls me Banty. They always have. I got that because I'm short. Like a banty rooster."

Deeana was so distraught that, upon Penelope's passing into slumber on this evening, Deeana roused herself and slipped next door to Herkimer's quarters. She rapped lightly on the door and, after a soft response to the question, "Who's there?" from inside, was admitted.

"What's wrong?" was Herk's opening remark.

"Nothing," she replied with a pleasant expression. "I just got lonely for your company. Penny is fast asleep and I—well I missed being in bed with you."

"But Penny ...?"

"She'll be fine. I locked the door. Here's the key. If she wakes up and cries we'll hear her. I'll get up in the night and go back in there."

Herkimer had been reading. He put the book aside and shifted so that a large portion of the double bed was left open for his spouse. The encounter was far less gratifying, however, than Deeana had anticipated. Herk remained distracted. She touched his shoulder and stroked his flank, but he did not respond.

"What's the matter, Sweetheart?" she asked.

"Nothing."

"But you seem so...so distant, almost cold."

"I'm sorry. I guess I'm just depressed.

"I thought we came out here so you—so all of us—might be renewed."

He was silent, looking away from her toward the emptiness of the seedy, little room.

"I feel worse," he said at length. "I come here and see the fertility of the land, breath the freshness of the air, and I just think of all I gave up to be in that...that...rat race back there."

"But you've got me and Penelope. We'll go anyplace with you. We'll live wherever you wish."

He turned to her now and gazed at her but with no comfort in his aspect and said, "Thank you, my Dear," then turned on his side away from her and clicked off the light.

A dejected Deeana turned away also and wept silently into her pillow. After a time, sufficient she thought, to allow him sleep, she arose and returned to the quarters she shared with their daughter.

The following morning, after an ample breakfast, Herk ushered them into the van and announced that they would make a visit to The Home Place, that square mile of land where, in the 1860's, Herk's great grandfather had settled subsequent to the Civil War. It was four miles from the town, across beautiful, rolling hills, the prevalent corn fields interrupted now and again by meadows the soulful purple of clover, the glowing gold of Spanish Bayonet. They approached the farm on a rough gravel road and arrived at an aging house set on a hill before a hen yard with white shed and sided by a barnyard with a large, red barn.

They pulled up into a drive alongside the house and as Herk descended from the van a door at the rear of the house opened and a large woman stepped out. She approached with a quizzical expression, scrutinizing Herk. As she came nearer her face broadened in a smile.

"Is that you, Banty?" she called.

"It is, indeed, Helga," he answered, smiling for the first time that day.

"Well, whata ya know!" she exclaimed as she took his hand firmly. "Herschel is down to the barn." She stepped back a pace and looked at him. "You always look good—like you ain't changed atall."

"Thanks," he said trying another weak grin. "This is my wife, Deeana, and my daughter, Penelope," he added, turning toward the van as the two stepped out. "This is Helga Wildt."

They greeted her agreeably, Deeana voicing a countrified, "Pleased ta meecha."

"Banty had to show you The Home Place, did he?" Helga said, extending her puffy cheeks in a grin. "Well, it was in his family for a long spell."

Herkimer escorted the girls down an incline, through the barnyard gate, to the large barn where they found Herschel Wildt forking hay from the mow into the cattle troughs below.

Wildt, too, was very large—it seemed most people in this Arcadia were over-eaters—and sported an expansive moustache, gray as was his hair. He had, for decades, tilled and nurtured these acres, sharing in the largess with The Judge. While The Judge had willed the property to his only son, as we have seen, Herkimer, in no need of funds, and not desirous of the concern, had deeded it over to its long term caretaker. Wildt was now the owner of the land he had cultivated for so long.

After Herkimer had introduced his family, Wildt asked, "How does it look, Banty?"

"It looks great, Herschel. I'm at a point in my life now where everything out here in the country feels good to me."

"Well, it ain't easy to maintain a family farm no more, what with all the big companies ownin' more and more of the land."

"That's just awful," Herk said. "Family farms built this country."

Deeana heard all this with curiosity. Herk's mood did not indicate this attitude he expressed. If he felt so good why didn't he show it? Or was it that he was just weary of his family, that she, because she was associated only with his experiences in the more sophisticated East, seemed little more than a burden to him. She was quite disturbed and masked her displeasure in irony.

"I'm glad you feel so well," she said to Herk, a grin on her face. "Maybe we can go to a concert tonight. Or the theater?"

"That'll be kinda hard around here," said a grinning Herschel. "Reckon you'll have to go back East for that. We got some good restaurants though. Ya oughta try *Hopkins'*. Virgil—that's Virgil Hopkins, the owner—he does serve the best home fries around. His steaks are mighty big and tasty, too."

"Good," said Deeana, still smiling as she turned to Herk. "Maybe you can take us there tonight."

"Yeah," said Herk, not smiling, sensing her disdain. "But first I want to look around the farm—if Herschel doesn't mind." He looked a question at the fat man.

"Not atall," Herschel said. "It's only 'cause a you—and your dad—that we got it. Hell, that we got anythin' atall."

They walked out, back of the house, to a gate which ran between two lines of fence, and looked down on a sizable pond of water in a kind of bowl created by the slopes of pasture surrounding it.

"I learned how to fish right down there—in that pond," Herk said looking down and smiling at Penny. He leaned over and raised her to his shoulders, legs to either side of his neck, and started back toward the car.

"We'll just drive down the road. It cuts the land in the middle. We'll stop over there on the hill and you can go out and see what it's like to romp in a field of clover."

They bid adieu to Herschel, Herk assuring him they would meet again before they left the environs of Clayton, and as they were proceeding to back down the drive in the van Helga leaned from the doorway, waved and called, "Come back before ya go, Banty."

After positive assurance that they would meet again Herk negotiated the driveway and turned onto the road, heading down a short incline then up another. There, they pulled to the shoulder and stopped. To one side was a field of corn, each stalk of equal height just above the fence line, to the other a field of green clover sprinkled with violet from myriad blossoms, almost the appearance of a Van Gogh or Monet painting.

They alighted from the van and strolled to the fence. Once again Herk lifted his daughter to his chest.

"Look, Sweetheart," he said. "There's your field of clover."

"Beautiful," came the voice of Deeana from just behind them, and Herk turned and, finally, cast, directly to her, a smile of some warmth.

"I always liked clover fields," he said with a smile and, walking down the fence line, he came to a place where wooden steps mounted the barrier and lead down the other side to the field. Deeana followed and they crossed into the leafy mead.

Herk lowered Penelope to the earth where she stood amongst the flowering plants which were waist high. As Penny walked out into the leafy bed her parents inspected the grounds. Running along the edge, between fence and field they saw, at perhaps fifty foot intervals, large ricks of wood, the remnants of small trees, it appeared, piled in perfect symmetry like little huts.

"Why are those piles of wood there?" asked Deeana.

"Oh," said Herk, a bit taken aback. "Oh..." And suddenly he remembered. "They'll burn those so the smoke will rid the field of chinch bugs. Some time in August the bugs come in so strong they can make a mess of everything. You ought to see them. They're thick like small clouds. The smoke from wood fires will chase them away."

"I thought they had sprays for things like that," Deeana wondered.

"Sometimes the old ways are the best ways," said Herk. "It's clean. No danger of harm as there is with so many of those sprays. Rachel Carson warned us, didn't she?"

Deeana nodded. "I see. They had a way to do it before DDT." She smiled at her new knowledge.

Penelope was delighted with her chance to play in the clover and returned with a bouquet of clover blossoms which she presented her mother.

Herkimer seemed more serene on their short trip back to the motel. On the way he pointed to a farm house where one of his boyhood friends had lived and seemed to enjoy the nostalgia this prompted.

"Are we going to Virgil's restaurant, tonight?" Deeana asked as they pulled into the lot at their lodgings.

Herk was at first puzzled but then he recalled what Herschel had said.

"Oh, you mean *Hopkins'*." He grinned. "You really want to try their home fries?"

"No," she said, "but maybe it will beat the diner."

They did enjoy their dinner at *Hopkins'*, Penny especially, for they served her a large dish of red gelatin as a starter and feted her further with a Sunday of vanilla ice cream topped with hot fudge. Herkimer, however, was still somewhat distant. Though he smiled at them it was not his usual sincere smile.

"What is the matter, Dear," Deanna asked when Penny had been bedded and the two sat on a bench between the two motel rooms they occupied. "You seem so unhappy."

For a moment Herk was silent, cogitating.

"I suppose," he said at length, "it is being here where I started. I think of all the hope I had then. The world was open ahead, and I meant to go out and conquer it. Look how completely I have botched my life." He leaned forward, elbows on his knees, and put his head in his hands, covering his eyes as though to close out all reality.

"Penelope and me? I suppose we're botches. Or is bitches better?" Her annoyance was evident in the tone of her voice. "You've scarcely taken notice of us all day long. Penny some, but I might as well not have been here."

He raised his head, now, but looked straight ahead. There was, for Deeana, a strained moment before he turned to her and said, softly, "I'm sorry. I really do love you, and I appreciate your putting up with me."

She reached out to him, took his hand and said, "Thank you, Dear Heart. I needed that." She held his hand a few more moments while they made compassionate eye contact. Then she said, softly as he had, "Let's get some sleep. Maybe you'll feel better tomorrow."

She arose, tugging him to his feet, and led him to his room. She went in with him and, for a long moment they clutched each other, body to body. Then she kissed him; he responded, and, after another lengthy gaze into one another's eyes, she turned and went to the room where their child slept. As she lay in her bed awaiting slumber she had a sudden recollection: the small phial presented to her by the strange, small man in the herbal store. Perhaps this is the type of situation to which he referred when he presented her the potion. She determined that she would give it a try. She would mix it with Herkimer's coffee on the morrow. It couldn't hurt. It was, after all, from a natural food shop.

XVI

Next morning, while devouring pancakes and sausage at the diner near the motel, Herk announced his intention to visit his mother's house and Ms. Hepzibah North so that he might retrieve a pair of hooked rugs of his mother's design. Deeana was determined, more even than before, to minister Wilkie's potion to her spouse. She volunteered to transport Herk's empty coffee to the counter and request a re-fill. When he acceded she took both his cup and hers to the woman behind the counter and requested refills.

"I'll bring them over to your table," said the pleasant server.

"No, I'll wait and take them," Deeana said, and, while the woman was at the coffee maker, removed the small phial from a pocket in her jeans and uncapped it.

The woman returned with the steaming cups and Deeana immediately asked if they might have two tiny containers of cream. As the woman turned away Deeana dumped a good portion of the contents of the phial into one cup, gave it a quick stir and, having received the cream capsules, returned to the table placing the tainted coffee before her husband. She watched as first he sipped then drained the liquid from his cup.

"That coffee was a little strong," was the only observation Herk made.

Deeana had been inclined to forego the visit to the house, but now she had begun to worry over the possible affect of her ministration and professed a desire to visit Herk's original home once again. She was, of course, immediately offended by the sight of Ms. North and even more so by the older woman's banter with "my Banty." The rugs in question, however, were of such interesting design that their appearance assuaged, somewhat, her pique.

She did feel that she perceived some alteration in Herk's conduct as they sat at the large, old dining table sipping tea which Ms. North had prepared for them. He began to scratch at his legs and to forget, half way through a sentence, the thought which he wished to express.

"When I was a kid," he said at one point, "I loved to ..." and his mind seemed to drift away to another thought before he could finish the sentence.

Had Deeana not accompanied him it is doubtful that the two rugs would have made it to the motel. Herkimer was quite distracted. He turned the wrong direction when they came to the highway on which the motel was situated. Deeana had to correct him. It was only with her sense of direction that they were able to return to their lodging. Herkimer was in that state of distraction.

The itch in his legs had spread to the upper reaches of his body and he was furiously scratching his torso when they reached the motel. It was past mid-day. They had lunched, thanks to the propriety of Ms. North who had afforded them a meal of chicken salad and home baked bread. Herkimer was alternately silent and distracted and maniacally loquacious.

"When I get hold of that damned Barber I'll cool him off!" he would exclaim, slipping into a past period of his life. Or, "That snake Fahtah will be sorry he ever met me."

Little Penelope, while confused by her father's flights into the past, was also amused at some of his actions. At one point, after they had arrived back at the motel, he flung himself to the grass and rolled about, buffing his body on the turf.

Deeana was terrified and full of remorse. She guessed that these reactions were caused by the potion with which she had defiled his coffee, but she must maintain a placid appearance for the sake of the child.

"Dear," she said to the wild man as he lay on the ground beneath her, "Why don't you go into your room and rest. Penny and I will go to the Pharmacy and get some lotion for your itch."

He did not appear to have heard her, but he arose from the turf and proceeded toward the motel room muttering, "That bastard Cerebino! I'll get him!"

After directing him into the proper room, Deeana took Penelope in the van and they went to the pharmacy where she purchased a bottle of lotion, advertised on the container as being a balm for itchy skin, and returned to the motel. With no objection from Herk she stripped him and applied the lotion over his entire frame. This seemed, for the moment, to assuage some of her husband's anguish and with the little one in hand she repaired to the office of the motel in search of aid. Herkimer was in need of the medical assistance only a doctor could provide. But, as she was receiving the telephone directory from the motel proprietor, they heard the rumble of a motor and glanced out the window to see their van proceed, at high speed, out the drive and onto the highway, Herkimer at the wheel.

They were never to see the husband and father again. The itching of his skin had become a conflagration throughout his body, an unbearable agony.

The Wildt's, who had gone to town for the evening to enjoy a moving picture, returned, somewhat before midnight, to find one of their wooden ricks in the clover field flickering in the last minutes of vitality. On the shoulder of the road, outside the fence, was the Hampton's van. Near the dying embers was the gasoline container Herk had carried against any calamitous shortage of fuel. But it was not until the light of morning that Herschel, upon inspection, discovered in the ashes some coins, a brass belt buckle and a few bones which had resisted the flame, Herkimer's last remains. He had concocted, from the wood rick, his own funeral pyre.

Epilogue

The Wildt's buried the few bones they had taken from the pyre in a shallow furrow beside the remains of The Judge and his wife. The service was attended by but few: the Wildt's, Hepzibah North, a couple of men who had been school mates to Herkimer.

Deeana was so distraught it was necessary that Mrs. Wildt conduct her to the grave site, Penelope following. The compassionate Wildt, himself, drove the widow and child to the Wallis home on Lake Minnetonka, which was, henceforth, their residence.

Mr. Wallis had the contents of the New York apartment shipped to Minnesota where they dispensed with all but memorabilia of the marriage. But Deeana remained distracted, speaking scarcely to anyone, not even her child, until, some months later, she disappeared. She did not surface until after Spring thaw, when her body was discovered, washed up onto the shore of the lake a short distance down from the Wallis' landing. The event was judged a suicide.

Penelope was embraced into the home of her grandparents where they bestowed upon her the same care and affection they had afforded her mother. She was a melancholy child, given to extensive periods of solitude on the expansive lawn beside the tranquil waters of the lake. On still nights of full moon she would carry with her the heirloom sword, raised triumphantly heavenward, where, she announced to her grandparents, she could perceive, in the translucent clouds, the face of her father, gazing down upon her with beatitude.